Ferdinand Dennis was born in Kingston, Jamaica, and spent the second half of his childhood in London. He studied at the University of Leicester and Birkbeck College, University of London. His work has been much anthologised, and he has contributed to many newspapers and magazines, including the *Guardian*, *Granta*, the *New Statesman* and the *Voice*. He lives in London.

THE BLACK AND WHITE MUSEUM

Stories by
Ferdinand Dennis

SMALL ✖ AXES

HopeRoad Publishing
PO Box 55544
Exhibition Road
London SW7 2DB

www.hoperoadpublishing.com
@hoperoadpublish

A CIP catalogue record for this book is available from the British Library

Supported using public funding by
**ARTS COUNCIL
ENGLAND**

ISBN: 978-1-913109-83-7
e-ISBN: 978-1-913109-17-2

Printed and bound by Clays Ltd, Elcograf S.p.A

For

A.D.S.D

Contents

Author's Note

These stories were conceived or written over the past five decades. An avid and even promiscuous reader of short stories – de Maupassant, Somerset Maugham, Gabriel Garcia Marquez, John Cheever, Doris Lessing and William Trevor authored some of my favourite examples of this much under-appreciated literary genre – I always envisaged publishing one day a collection of my own, so freshly minted stories were often filed away for years before once more seeing the light of day. There were, for example, at least twelve years between writing 'Wet Sunday Morning Blues' and its publication in an anthology; and 'Christmas Fire', though written in the early 1990s, makes its debut in this collection. The title story, 'The Black and White Museum', written later in the 1990s and published twice during that decade, was inspired by my experience of living in a certain south-west English city with a strong slave-trading past. It was my attempt, irreverent and humorous, yet somehow deadly serious, to cope with that city's ubiquitous and oppressive reminders of its history. 'Nine Night' was specially written for this collection.

The Black and White Museum

It was originally called the Emporium, and while it bore that name it remained a curious but much underused retail outlet on Kingsland High Street in Hackney. During those early days its proprietor, Papa Legba, could often be seen standing at its glass door looking wistfully at the indifferent passers-by making their way to McDonald's, Kentucky Fried Chicken, Ridley Road market or the shopping arcade. The Emporium's crowded and chaotic window display of books, plaster icons, bottled herbs and lucky charms was not on anybody's shopping list.

Papa Legba was new to the retailing business, but he was no fool. Short and stocky, with a complexion similar to the colour of cinnamon bark, he always wore a white kaftan, and his thick convex spectacles, slight stoop, huge forehead and head of untidy grey hair gave him an air of owlish wisdom. There was substance to this appearance. Papa Legba had travelled to many lands and possessed the gift of tongues. He spoke flawless English, all the major European languages and so many African languages that he himself often forgot his knowledge of a tongue until somebody addressed him in it. After much thought over several warm spring nights, Papa Legba decided that the Emporium's shortage of customers was due to its lack of a clear-cut identity. So he renamed it 'the Black and White Museum'.

Within twenty-four hours of his effecting this name change Papa Legba's establishment began to reap the rewards. A steady stream of customers wandered in. They browsed through the books, which were stacked in floor-to-ceiling wall shelves and ranged from Alex Haley's *Roots* to antique tomes with titles like *Stolen History* and *Narrative of a Survivor of the Middle Passage*; some were brand new, their stiff virginal spines waiting to be broken in by their readers; others were dog-eared with yellowing mildewed pages and reeked of abandonment.

Several notices on the bookshelves invited customers to borrow books for a token fee and proof of their name and address; for a small deposit, any book published anywhere in Africa or the African diaspora over the past fifty years could be ordered in and delivered within a month; three months for anything older.

But the Black and White Museum was far more than a bookshop. Its back room was a bazaar of African artefacts: ebony masks; statuettes made from ivory and ebony, iroko walking sticks, malachite brooches, earrings, necklaces and bracelets; bronze replicas of the Benin mask; fertility dolls from Kenya and Zimbabwe; metal horns from Hausa land; marimbas from the Cameroon; cloths with elaborate patterns from the Congo; Lagos- and Dakar-designed clothes in indigo and gold; and seashell necklaces from a small village on the Guinea coast where it was believed the shells contained the souls of Enslaved Africans who had drowned themselves rather than suffer the horror of the Middle Passage. A notice above the doorway leading to the back room read: 'Please feel free to browse'. Like other notices in the shop it was signed *Mr P. Legba*.

Papa Legba was very generous to these early customers. If a book, a carving or a piece of jewellery caught somebody's fancy, he charged only what the purchaser could afford. Urging them to take the item, he would beam on these customers a most beautiful smile of perfect white teeth – which were either dentures, expensive crowns or the result of orthodontic knowledge unknown to the rest of mankind – and he would say to these sceptical customers: 'It's your history, pay me what you can.'

Soon word of Papa Legba's kindness began to circulate, but it was satisfied customers who really brought the Black and White Museum fame. Hortense Smith was one of the early enthusiasts. The long-suffering Jamaican mother of six children, she chanced upon the Black and White Museum on a summer day when she was going through one of the periodically difficult phases that had been marking her life since she married Leroy Smith, a shiftless, drunken, foul-mouthed, violent womaniser. Not being much of a book reader, she wandered to the back of the shop and there discovered a small recess crammed with glass jars containing a variety of herbs for physical ailments such as arthritis, lumbago, eczema and psoriasis; dried barks from the baobab, fruits for curing emotional problems such as bereavement and troubled hearts. There were toxic powders for eliminating tyrannical spouses or lovers, zombie powder for zombifying your enemies, dried leaves for courage, and herbs that gave you freedom.

Hortense Smith expressed interest in some straight-back grass, a herb that the label on the jar informed her was particularly effective for reforming wayward husbands. Papa Legba weighed out four ounces on a gold scale and instructed Hortense to grind it up into a powder, then mix the powder with skin shed by her husband and boil for three hours. The brew created through this process should then be consumed by the subject within the next twenty-four hours. If, after a month, she wasn't happy with the result – an industrious, faithful, home-loving husband – Papa Legba promised to give her a complete refund.

Hortense Smith returned five weeks later looking younger and happier and gushing with praise for the straight-back grass she had purchased. It had not only turned her errant husband into a temperate, affectionate companion, it had made him into something of a sexual athlete submissively responsive to the starting pistol of her physical desires. She was accompanied by two friends, Mildred Marshall and Esther Harris, who wanted some of what Hortense had bought, the exact same thing. These satisfied customers became walking, talking adverts for the Black and White Museum.

Soon customers started arriving from all over London. Some days a long queue stretched as far as Ridley Road market; people even stood for hours in the rain and cold for the opportunity to purchase the museum's potent panaceas. Naturally once they were inside the shop they became curious about its other goods, the books and the African artefacts. And when they had bought their herbs along with, say, a pair of ivory earrings or a goatskin drum, some noticed the red arrow pointing to the basement and the words 'The Middle Passage'.

Initially only the most intrepid customers ventured down the slimy rickety wooden stairs. At the bottom they found hundreds of yards of rough-cast iron chains, padlocks, leg-clamps, neck-locks, neck-rings in various styles, iron masks, cat-o'-nine tails, branding irons, wooden clamps and leather thongs, sweat boxes, treadmills and torture racks. Everything was encrusted with dried blood. A notice invited customers to take advantage of a special introductory rate for the 'Middle Passage Weekend'.

The first fifty adventurous souls, an equal mixture of blacks and whites, had a hell of a time. For forty-eight hours they lay on their backs, head to toe, side by side, in a dank, damp fetid sub-basement. By some hidden mechanical device the sub-basement floor simulated the rolling and listing of a slave ship in the Middle Passage. It was mercilessly hot and every hour, on the hour, sprinklers built into the ceilings sprayed the visitors with cold salt water. And throughout all this, the pain-filled voices of men, women and children issued from concealed loudspeakers. Once a day Papa Legba served a meal of foul-smelling grub-infested gruel. A few traumatised adventurers emerged babbling in strange languages, some of which defied even Mr Legba's encyclopaedic linguistic knowledge. To aid their recovery he sold them sachets of dried elephants' brains, which he assured them would restore their memory of who they were before the Middle Passage Weekend. But the majority of people not only walked away unhurt, they claimed it had been a uniquely invigorating, even cathartic, experience.

Indeed, one Englishman, who was married to a Dominican, was so moved that when he had stopped shaking his head and muttering, 'The horror, the horror, I didn't know,' he turned to a group of black men and asked them for forgiveness.

The Nigerian answered: 'Forgiveness? I was hoping you might go into partnership. We have many cities in my country that are overcrowded with Osus. They'll soon need labour on the Moon or Mars – you can take them there.'

The Trinidadian in the group said: 'Forgiveness? Sure, man. Let we get some women, a bottle a rum and go jump up at carnival.'

The Guyanese said: 'Sure, I'll forgive you. But we have to negotiate forgiveness. Let's talk about reparation.'

The Barbadian said, with great nobility and magnanimity: 'That's history; the soil from which a better tomorrow may grow. There's nothing to forgive.'

The Jamaican, when asked for forgiveness by the Englishman, said: 'Forgive you? Me would never forgive you, not on the beaches, not in the fields, not in the hills.' He then threw a wild punch at the Englishman and had to be restrained by his friends.

The Jamaican's name was Winston Hill and the Middle Passage Weekend was something of a life-changing experience for him. He gave up his job with British Telecom, bolted some steel doors on his twentieth-floor apartment overlooking Hackney Downs, started growing dreadlocks, and turned his flat into a pirate radio station called Maroons FM. It played nothing but plugs for the Black and White Museum, and juju, dub and Nyabinghi music interspersed with the terrifying sound of Mau Mau warriors initiating new recruits. Unfortunately Winston Hill's Maroons FM kept on drifting into the same frequency as Radio Three, and after much protest from that station's outraged and influential listeners, the authorities started a campaign to close it down without offending its thousands of black listeners and risking a riot.

First they tried to trick him. They wrote to Mr Hill informing him that he would have to move as they were planning to demolish the high-rise block where he lived. Winston Hill wrote back saying that they should go ahead and demolish the other nineteen floors and leave him where he was. Eventually, Chief Inspector Blair Orwell, leading what became known as Operation Big Brother, succeeded in removing Winston Hill from his apartment and silencing Maroons FM. Winston Hill was given a choice between going into a mental asylum or being deported to another country. He chose to be deported to somewhere in Africa but within a month he turned up at Heathrow Airport claiming refuge from the madness he had witnessed in Ajegunle, Lagos, Nigeria.

Cyril Baker had heard about the Black and White Museum on Maroons FM. A fat, timid filing clerk who had daily and stoically endured racial abuse from his colleagues and neighbours, Cyril Baker first visited Papa Legba's establishment to buy an extract of lion's heart to give him courage. After several doses had failed to rid Cyril of his cowardice, Papa Legba persuaded him to try the Middle Passage Weekend. It worked. He emerged leaner, fitter and mean: very mean. On his first day back at work Cyril wore a T-shirt bearing the message: *I survived the Middle Passage, so don't fuck with me.* Some months later Cyril gave up his job, became Papa Legba's unpaid assistant and dedicated his time to publicising the Black and White Museum.

Cyril's publicity efforts, combined with those of Maroons FM, brought so many enthusiastic customers for the Middle Passage Weekend that Papa Legba became greedy. He began to ignore the maximum capacity of the sub-basement, which was seventy-five. On a Carnival weekend, he packed three hundred people in there. This feat was achieved by building four new layers of shelves, thus heightening the authenticity of the Middle Passage experience. Sadly, thirty people almost suffocated to death in one session, forcing the proprietor to once again observe the maximum number. Far from adversely affecting the attendance, that near-fatal mishap blessed the Black and White Museum with notoriety, which boosted the number of visitors. Whole families booked in for the weekends and people came back for second and third trips. Like earlier visitors, they claimed it helped to soothe some troubled part of their psyche. Mr Legba took their money and smiled his beautiful smile.

After a while, the impact of the Black and White Museum began to be seen way beyond its modest high-street site. Children on nearby housing estates replaced familiar games like doctors and nurses with new ones like slave and slave master. And it inspired a new style of clothes. Young men and women could been seen on street corners in ragged half-length trousers, shredded shirts, iron necklaces that hung down to the ground, leg-clamps and leg-chains attached to iron balls or chunks of logs. The wealthier exhibitionists favoured tattered linen and silk, and gold- and silver-plated chains. Couples showed their affection for each other by chaining themselves together. The nightclubs now sweated to new dance crazes like 'the lashing', which involved one dancer holding a cat-o'-nine tails and pretending to whip the other dancer who twisted and writhed in rhythmic pretend agony. Another dance was called 'Escape' and entailed the dancer dashing about wildly with bulging eyes apparently streaming with tears of terror. The strangest of these dance-hall trends, though, was the 'Middle Passage Bogle', in which the dancer lay on the floor, hands pressed to his side, convulsing madly and frothing at the mouth, and all in perfect timing to the furiously bass-filled music known as jungle.

Now, of course, it's well known that black folk are major trendsetters in Western popular culture. What black youths wear on the streets today is seen on the catwalks tomorrow; the music they listen to in obscure nightclubs is heard on mainstream pop shows months later. So it won't surprise you to hear that white folk soon started copying the street trends inspired by the Black and White Museum. An ambitious starlet outraged television viewers when she appeared on an early evening chat show wearing crystal earrings in the shape of Ashanti fertility dolls and a dress of rusting chains that concealed little of her delightful body. That triggered a craze for similarly risqué dresses and skirts in what became known as 'the slave style', though more polite circles preferred the euphemism 'ethnic'.

When a disgruntled pop musician branded his forehead with the name of the record company that had tricked him into signing a ten-year contract, the entire music industry was swept with slave fever. Several successful new groups were launched. One consisted of four young men from Manchester known as 'Al White and the Oyinbo Posse'. They had an international hit with 'Mother Africa', a terrible ballad lamenting mankind's centuries-old exile from the Edenic conditions of the Rift Valley. Another group, 'Wazungu with Attitude', had a phenomenally huge one-off rap hit with a repetitive song called 'The Atlantic Crossing'. They subsequently disappeared, leaving rumours that they had drowned themselves in the Atlantic Ocean, though two members of the band were spotted, some months later, in a brothel in Mombasa, Kenya.

The manufacturers of a well-known brand of sports shoes got in on the act with trainers known as the

'Plantation' – an especially rugged and heavy footwear, which, by some curious device, made a rattling noise as the wearer walked. Not to be outdone, their closest market rival launched the 'Runaway', with a multi-million-pound advertising campaign using Linford Christie dressed in shredded electric-blue Lycra tights and wearing the eponymous trainers, which were distinguishable from those of their rivals by foot-long chains attached to the heels.

Meanwhile, back on the streets, black folk – perhaps feeling that their culture had once again been stolen – were finding new styles and fashions. The Black and White Museum, the unacknowledged inspiration behind dance, music and clothes styles, suffered a reversal of fortune. Fickle fashion had moved on and, one November evening, Papa Legba closed its doors to the general public for the last time. He sold his entire stock to a forward-looking Jamaican-Jewish businessman, Carl Spencer Marks, who believed that history always repeats itself, the first time as tragedy, the second time as farce and the third time as retro-fashion.

The site where the Black and White Museum once stood is now a huge restaurant specialising in nouvelle soul food. Hortense Smith is now the Conservative MP for Milton Keynes. Cyril Baker is now Head of the Universal African Church of Revelation and Redemption, which has branches in Liverpool, Bristol, Greenwich and the Shetland Islands. Winston Hill is now, reportedly, an illegal immigrant in Brooklyn, New York, where he belongs to a fast-growing sect that regards Cuba as Zion,

Fidel Castro as God and Bill Gates, the head of Microsoft, as the Antichrist.

As for Papa Legba himself, he was last sighted in the Bahamas, where he is believed to be investigating the scientific and commercial potential of the humble banana for producing an intelligence-boosting drug.

Father and Daughter

Michael Welles was sitting in the arrivals lounge at Gatwick Airport on a grey autumn day waiting for his daughter, whom he had never met before. She was the legacy of the only foreign holiday he had ever taken in his life – a visit to his maternal grandparents in Jamaica, resulting in the fling that made him a parent. Still, he had tried to do the right thing within the limits of his resources; he remitted money monthly, acknowledged her birthdays. When the child, approaching adolescence and capable of writing long fluent letters, started appealing to him to be brought to Britain, he resolved to grant her request. It would take him almost a decade to find his way through the labyrinth of UK immigration rules.

The plane arrived, but it seemed to take forever for the passengers to start emerging from the arrivals path. Eventually, three passengers with bottles of Jamaica rum in cartons sauntered out and after a pause more followed. Michael became aware of his shaking legs and sweaty palms, the effect of the countless cups of coffee he had drunk while waiting, having arrived at the airport far too early. Then the trickle became a flood as men, women and children carrying holiday souvenirs began to appear. He checked the photograph of Lena that he was carrying against passengers he thought might be her, then his attention weakened and all females faces, young and old, merged and blurred into one.

When a female voice said, 'Michael Welles?' and he found himself gazing down into the brown eyes of a young woman who looked like a younger version of his long-departed grandmother, he could only stutter an indecisive, uncertain, 'Yes.'

'Daddy,' she said and threw herself at him, clinging to him with a force inspired by the terror and relief of arrival.

'Lena,' he said, hugging the jeans-clad young woman who he had up until now known only in photographs, letters and fuzzy international telephone calls.

The journey back to Michael's home in Hackney took almost two hours on the M25. Rain fell occasionally and the November landscape had a cold, austere beauty to it. Lena slept through most of the journey, coiled up on the front seat. As they entered Homerton High Street, Michael became aware that she was awake and looking out of the car window.

'Is it what you expected?' he asked.

'I didn't know what to expect,' she said.

He brought her to his one-bedroom basement flat off Stoke Newington High Road. He had painted the bedroom pale red, bought a new dresser and wardrobe, put up new curtains and laid down oak-effect laminate flooring. He would sleep in the living room on a foldaway bed kept in a hallway cupboard.

'I've never had a room of my own,' she said.

Michael knew from Lena's letters that her mother had three other children and that the father of one of her siblings lived in the USA.

Over dinner that evening, he presented her with a set of keys, and a copy of the London A-Z.

She said, 'Thank you, Daddy.'

Michael felt uncomfortable being called Daddy and told her so. 'Call me Mike or Michael,' he suggested. 'That's what most people call me, Mike or Michael.'

'But I'm not most people,' she said, smiling. She explained that her half-brother's father was a constant visitor in her mother's house and she envied the boy having someone to call Daddy and longed with all her heart to address, face to face, her own Daddy. 'I brought this for you, Daddy,' she said. 'I picked the beans myself.' She presented him with a bag of ground coffee. 'And these are some photos we took on Emancipation Day. We were in Kingston for a week.'

Michael took the bundle of photos and examined them slowly. When he came to a picture of Lena with an older woman standing below a large sculpture of a naked couple, he asked, 'Who's the lady?'

'That's my mother.'

He heard a quiet indignation in her voice. The photo of Lena's mother brought back memories of that fateful month-long holiday in Portland, and the afternoon spent under the jackfruit tree with a girl who worked as a domestic in a neighbouring house.

Disconcerted, he looked at Lena, then the thought came to him that this young woman would be the only evidence that he had lived, just as he was the only proof of his mother's life, though he was sure that his father, whoever and wherever he was, had fathered many children. She was quite right: she wasn't just most people. She was his only child.

That night, he sat in his living room listening to a stranger, his daughter, move around his flat as she prepared for bed. When he heard her lock the bedroom door and switch off the light, he prepared for bed himself. He found the bathroom cleaner than he had ever seen it, and smelling of talcum powder, which was oddly disturbing and pleasing. He brought out the foldaway bed, with the bedding, and set it up in the living room. At some point in the night, he woke up startled, wondering why he was sleeping in his living room.

Over the next month Michael showed Lena around London. He took her for drives on the North Circular and across the river, they went for rides on the Underground and on the buses, and he introduced her to Ridley Road market. For immigration purposes she was here to further her studies and Michael was paying, something he could afford to do with his wages as a cabinet-maker combined with an inheritance from his mother. She had recently passed away and left him a small sum of money, which Michael had wanted to invest in buying his own flat but decided instead to grant his daughter's wish to live in England. The sooner she enrolled on a course the better.

During the next five years Michael shared his home with Lena, his daughter. He ensured there was always food in the house and stifled any resentment he felt at the rate at which she got through sugar and fruit juice, the length of time she took in the bathroom, the nights she came in late without calling to let him know she would not be home for dinner. He sought consolation from the knowledge that she was serious about her studies and worked part-time in a Caribbean bakery store in West Green Road to help pay her way. Each year she successfully passed exams until she graduated with a BA degree in Management Studies from London Metropolitan University.

Soon after she started working for a travel agency, Michael and Lena were having dinner one Sunday, when she said: 'There's something I have to tell you, Daddy. I'm seeing a guy.'

'You are?'

'Yes.'

'Is it serious? Is *he* serious?'

'Yes. He's asked me to marry him?'

Michael almost choked on his food. 'Marry him?'

'Yes.'

'Am I going to meet this young man?' Michael asked, suddenly feeling older than his years.

'Yes.' Lena took out her mobile and moved her fingers at lightning speed to send a text. 'He's outside waiting. Can he come in?'

'Course,' Michael said.

Lena's fiancé was called Barry and he was born in Luton and worked as a British Telecom engineer.

Michael gave the couple his blessing. Lena soon moved out, and a few months later, on a warm Saturday in July,

he was the proudest father as he gave his daughter away at
the New Testament Church of God in Stoke Newington.

The next two years were punctuated with news of Lena's
miscarriages. She was passed from one medical specialist
to another; none found a physiological reason for her
inability to carry a pregnancy to full term.

Michael was always responsive to her tears. He went to
the couple's home, a ground-floor flat in Lower Clapton,
no matter how tired he was after work. He hugged and
comforted his daughter and reassured her that everything
would be all right.

On one of his visits after the third miscarriage,
Michael heard from Barry that Lena had got religion in
a serious way. 'Three times a week, she goes,' he said. 'All
day Sunday.'

'And you're not religious?'

'I married her for better or for worse.'

Michael left Lena and Barry's home thinking that she
was fortunate to have found a man like Barry.

Lena's fourth miscarriage was the worst. She was put
on medication, forced to stop work, and nothing Michael
did or said could ease her pain, which he felt so acutely
that he cried alone in his basement flat one night.

Soon after that, Michael discovered that Lena had
found a new church. Barry reported: 'She's tried quite a
few others, one in Finsbury Park, another in Seven Sisters.
Now she's trying one somewhere off the Old Kent Road.'

Barry looked worn out. Michael took him for a drink
at the White Hart pub.

'For better or worse,' Barry said as they parted.

One October Saturday afternoon Michael received a visit from Lena. He had not seen her for a few weeks, and was struck by how thin she looked.

'You're not eating right,' Michael said lightheartedly. He had cooked a pot of soup in anticipation of her visit. He filled a large bowl with the soup of mutton, yam, dasheen and cornmeal dumpling.

Lena said grace, then took a few mouthfuls, pushed the bowl aside and said, 'I've found a new church, Daddy.'

'That's great, Lena,' he said, and stifled his resentment at her rejection of the meal he had laboured over for hours.

'Thing is, they say ...' Lena swallowed her words and tears began to stream down her face.

Michael got up from his chair, went to her and placed an arm around her. 'Take your time, Lena,' he said. 'I'm right here, ba ...' he almost said 'baby' then caught himself. He had never called her baby.

Lena went to the bathroom and Michael could hear her blowing her nose.

She returned looking far more composed. She said, 'You know how much I want a child, Daddy. And Barry does, too.'

'Yes, I know, I know.'

'Well, in my new church – the church I found, the Church of Holy Light, the church I am going to – Pastor Ogbonni says the Lord will answer my prayer only when I give up something or someone that's precious to me.'

'You know I'm not religious, Lena. I've never heard of such a thing.'

'They say it works, Daddy. They say it works.'

Michael stared at her as the force of what she was implying struck him. Was she about to give up Barry, her husband? What kind of church would encourage a wife to leave her husband?

She rushed towards him, embraced him, kissed his cheek and said, 'I'm sorry, Daddy, I'm sorry.' Michael was so shocked, he couldn't move as she dashed out of the room and out of the flat.

Michael allowed a few days to pass before he telephoned Barry and they again met in the White Hart Pub.

'There's nothing I can do, Mike,' Barry said, repeating what he had said in their telephone conversation. 'She's convinced the Pastor at her new church is right, and nothing's going to change her mind. Who knows? Maybe it'll work.'

'You really believe that?'

'I said maybe. We've tried everything else. The doctors say there's nothing wrong with her. Maybe this will work. I don't know, Mike, I just don't know. And if it works, then I can't see any reason why you can't start visiting again.'

Michael had asked for this meeting with Barry in the hope of winning his support to help change Lena's mind. But he now heard in Barry's voice a desperation that made any proposed solution, no matter how wild, worth trying. He decided he would be tolerant and patient, give them time. And, as Barry said, if separation from him helped Lena, there was always afterwards. So he parted with

Barry amicably and told him he would respect Lena's wish and keep away from her.

But after a few weeks Michael's resolve weakened and he tried to make contact with Lena and Barry. When he discovered that both mobile numbers were no longer available, he drove to their home on a frosty December evening. He thought it strange that there was no light in the window. He pressed the doorbell but there was no answer. As he stood there a young man opened the front door. Michael asked, 'Do you know if Lena or Barry are around?'

'The couple on the ground floor? They moved out weeks ago, mate. Gone up north, I heard.'

Michael staggered backwards and almost fell over, and though he remained upright, he would never quite recover.

Nine Night

Wendell stepped out of Queen's Park tube station into a mild and dry late-January Saturday night, which made the greatcoat he was wearing feel unnecessary. He paused and felt a pang of apprehension, one of several since he had begun the journey, and was momentarily confused by a bank of luminous windows on a multi-storey building that was not part of his memory of the view from the station front. The building to the south of the railway bridge was grey and white, and it seemed to overhang the sunken railway tracks and hover above the ground; behind it was a cluster of 1960s tower blocks, more familiar landmarks. He checked his mobile phone for calls or messages he might have missed, then turned right and crossed the bridge over the railway lines. Within a few minutes he reached his destination, St Mark's Anglican Church.

People were milling about in the church's small car park. Among them he thought he recognised one of Dion's sisters in a group of women. He approached her, took off his cap, and felt the chill of the January night on his shaved head.

'Lilian?'

'Yes.' She was petite and brown, and in the light from the church building the changes wrought by the passing decades were evident – and yet there still remained in her middle-aged face the child he had known as Dion's little sister.

'Wendell Clarke.'

She searched his face for a second, then smiled in a way that was both vague and quizzical.

'My deepest sympathy,' he said.

Then she seemed to finally recognise him and stepped forward and thanked him, and they embraced briefly.

'Is that really you, Little Lilian?' he said with genuine affection and she laughed.

'I'm not so little any more,' she said, 'and I have got three kids and two grand-kids.'

She laughed again, as if this disclosure was a stock humorous response to people who insisted on always seeing her as Dion's little sister. Later that night, as the gathering sang, he would see her weeping and being comforted for having lost her only brother.

He asked after her elder sister, Patsy, and she told him that Patsy had long since returned to Jamaica. Then he asked after Irene, one of the sources of his earlier apprehension, and was told she would be along later. Lilian then said that she would see him inside and went back to join her friends. He wondered whether Irene looked like her younger sister, then remembered that each of Dion's three siblings had different fathers.

He proceeded into the church. He thought he recognised some of the people in the reception area, but could not place names to faces so settled for nodding and smiling. He got a bottle of water from behind the bar and took the only available seat beside a man with florid cheeks, sleepy brown eyes and slow speech. The man's name was John and they soon struck up a conversation.

'Did you know Dion well?' John asked.

Wendell told him that he and Dion, who had been a year older, had lived on the same street and attended the same secondary school. Wendell couldn't explain to this stranger the full connection between himself and Dion Granger, the many reasons he felt compelled to attend this Nine Night even though he hadn't seen Dion in over thirty years. He couldn't share his memory of their last encounter, on Kilburn High Road, he and Dion, the handsome muscular Adonis with a rich golden-brown complexion and an easy smile. Or the many other times from an earlier period, when Dion's older sister Patsy rented a room in Wendell's father's house, and when Dion invited him back to the Grangers' home to listen to music and played for him Led Zeppelin's 'Whole Lotta Love' and Delroy Wilson's 'Have Some Mercy' and 'Elizabethan Reggae' by Boris Gardiner. All this while Irene, on whom a pubescent Wendell had a crush, was somewhere else in the flat where Dion and his female siblings lived with their mute mother. He couldn't tell this stranger with the florid cheeks that Dion's family, also Jamaicans, were inseparable from his memories of his first decade in London.

And because he couldn't tell the stranger all these things, Wendell turned the question back to John.

John said he knew the family through their late mother who had been a stalwart of this church, and told Wendell how he had seen Dion weeks before he died in hospital of complications following chemotherapy for prostate cancer.

While Wendell and John were talking, the reception slowly filled up. Wendell saw many familiar faces from his childhood but none that he had known well. That changed within a few minutes with the entry of two classmates from his secondary school, Trevor Haynes and Stan Mason, who had told Dion about the event over the phone. Both Trevor and Stan had lived within a few hundred yards of Wendell's childhood home. He excused himself from John and went to join them.

Soon he was part of a group of sexagenarian men whose lives had started in Grenada, Barbados, Jamaica, Nevis, Dominica, St Lucia, Guyana and Nigeria. They had all been child migrants and so could recall their silent perplexity at the many seemingly dead trees in their first London winter, the novelty of duffel coats and scarves, and the enchantment of snow. Most had not seen each other in decades, but having once attended this church before discovering that the Methodist church five hundred yards away ran a better youth club, having played football on the surrounding streets and in the nearby park on long summer evenings, and having delivered newspapers together on cold winter mornings, they shared a past that made them members of an obscure and exclusive circle. Their stomachs were larger, their hair thinner and their faces less smooth; three had undergone surgery for fitting pacemakers and defibrillators and new hips. Their working lives as telephone engineers, car mechanics and builders were drawing to a close, and some were already grandfathers; at least one of them could become a great-grandfather before reaching his eighth decade.

When Trevor Haynes told Wendell not to use any fancy words on him, triggering laughter in the group, Wendell was reminded of his difference from these old school friends. The others had all left school at the earliest opportunity, but he had unexpectedly stayed on. While they were learning various trades as car mechanics in garages, on building sites and in telephone junction boxes, he had moved from classrooms to university lecture theatres, only starting work in his early twenties. Then a publishing house, long defunct, had published a small collection of his poetry – youthful verses about love and race and nostalgia. The muse had deserted him afterwards, but his education and the sole publication had earned him a curious respect that had survived both the barrenness that followed his early promise and his material poverty compared to these old friends. Their laughter made him feel that the closest he had to a home was this city and these men, and because his link to them was weak, he would soon only have this city and all the memories it held for him.

Wendell was talking to Derek Baptiste when he saw Stevie Johnson approaching. Stevie had a full head of thick greying hair that was part Afro and part dreadlocks. He was as slim as in his schooldays when he was a champion cross-country runner. Somebody had earlier told Wendell that as well as owning a thriving building company, Stevie had mastered several martial arts styles, earning himself the title of Grandmaster. Wendell straightened his back as Stevie moved through the group shaking hands. When he reached Wendell, he extended his hand but as Wendell, expecting a handshake, returned the gesture, Stevie Johnson pulled his hand away, leaving Wendell clutching at thin air. Then Stevie, eyes locked on Wendell, swayed from side to side, laughed and looked at the group of men. When nobody else laughed, Stevie stopped and said, 'I was only joking.'

'Knew you were joking,' Wendell said.

'Still serious, eh Wendell?'

They shook hands at last, and Stevie said: 'Heard you became a lecturer.'

'An administrator in education, that's all.'

'Still doing it?'

'No, took early retirement. And you, still in the building trade?'

'Yeah, yeah. Never done anything else.'

Just then, to Wendell's relief, Lilian announced that the service was starting, and people began filing into the hall. Someone called Stevie Johnson and he drifted away from Wendell who, during their brief exchange, had struggled to suppress the memories of the day he and Stevie fought in the school playground. He could not remember what had triggered the fight or even whether the fight had been conclusive; all he remembered was its aftermath, an all-consuming inner rage that filled his mind with murderous thoughts of revenge.

He had left the school premises, wandering alone around Paddington Green, then caught a number 18 bus outside the Odeon Cinema, alighting at the bus stop near the street where he lived. And all the while an inferno raged inside him and he silently swore to inflict the most terrible injuries on Stevie Johnson: he would blind him, deafen him, cut out his tongue, sever his limbs. He did not go home. He walked down Harrow Road, past the Ha'penny Steps, until he came to the redbrick Victorian building housing the Public Library. He entered the library and strolled among its shelves for a while before picking up a large picture book about sea creatures. And by the time he had finished leafing through it, mostly looking at the pictures, sometimes reading passages about dolphins or whales, he felt calmer.

It seemed to him that the shelves of books had in themselves generated a tranquility and silence that he had never before experienced, even though he had visited the library many times. He found another book, this time a collection of stories, and got so lost in reading them that he didn't hear the librarian call closing time. He left the building with great reluctance but the stillness and peacefulness of the library seemed to have entered his being and followed him home, and remained palpable even until the following morning. He never got into another playground fight.

Wendell got separated from his friends and went to stand on the far side of the hall, near the back. At the front of the hall a DJ stood among a small console and a tower of speaker boxes. Women, children and the less able-bodied men sat at the few tables. Like the rest of the building, the hall was cold and people kept their coats on. As he searched the hall for Irene, he realised he would probably not be able to recognise the woman whom he regarded as his first love.

The vicar, a tall gangly man, led a prayer and then a hymn. Wendell, fingers threaded, hands below his waist, eyes open but trained on the floor, tried to appear respectful of the proceedings. He had long ago stopped believing. He wondered how different his life would have been if, on that day nearly fifty years before, he had walked into a church and found inner peace among the vacant pews, under the gaze of the saints depicted in the stained-glass windows. Would he have become a priest? A purveyor of time-worn words for welcoming newborns, despatching the dead and consoling those who must live with their losses? And he was glad it had been the library and not the church he had wandered into, glad he had avoided the consolations of delusional religious dogma and found instead the wondrous uncertainty of knowledge.

The vicar must have noticed his detachment because later on he would glower at Wendell in a most un-Christian manner.

After the brief service, Wendell was introduced to Dion's ex-wife and two children. The wife was of Sierra Leonean and English parentage and carried herself with dignified solemnity. The daughter was a shy giant and the son, a professional footballer, was inseparable from his fiancée whose face was mostly hidden behind her long blonde hair. Stan Mason, who had told Wendell about the Nine Night, later revealed that Dion had cheated on his wife and she had thrown him out of the family home years before. Wendell felt a rush of sympathy for Dion, who after a fatherless childhood had succeeded in creating a model family of his own, but had fallen well short of perfection. And those good looks probably didn't help.

Back in the reception area, Wendell was catching up with Ken Davies when Lilian approached him and said, 'Irene is in the kitchen.'

He went there immediately.

The woman who stood in the centre of the kitchen under a fluorescent strip was a striking sight. She had her brother's and Lilian's golden-brown complexion, and wore a white turban-style hat, large disc-shaped gold earrings and a blue ankle-length coat, and when she laughed, her golden molars flashed. To Wendell's consternation, he did not recognise her, would have walked past her on the street. As a thirteen-year-old girl, she gave him his first kiss and she had remained frozen in his memory as his first love – but now, a half-century later, he could see no traces of the child in this woman.

'Irene?'

'Yes.'

'Wendell Clarke,' he said.

'Oh, my God! Wendell Clarke!'

'Long time.'

They hugged, gazed into each other's eyes for a heartbeat, then hugged again, this time for a second or two longer than the first.

He could not remember her being quite the same shade as her brother, and only when he caught a glimpse of her hands, a shade or two darker than her face, did he realise that the golden complexion was probably chemically induced rather than inherited. Nonetheless he could not deny that the woman standing before him radiated health and affluence, and confidence.

She told him she was a mother of two and a grandmother, and had spent her working life, which began early because she had to help her mother pay the bills, in retailing female accessories, designer handbags and fashion jewellery. She didn't say where, but he wondered whether she had worked in one of the department stores on Oxford Street, asked himself whether he had seen her but failed to recognise her among the immaculately groomed women who served in those shops.

'That explains those magnificent ear clips,' he said.

'These are not definitely not fashion jewellery,' she said, laughing her golden laugh.

Just then Stevie Johnson joined them.

'Hello, Stevie,' she said, switching her attention to the newcomer. 'Do you remember Wendell?'

'Yeah, yeah. Course, course, we were in school together. Same school as Dion.'

'Oh yeah, I forgot. So many of you guys went to that school.'

'And you were at Hodgkins School, other side of Paddington Green.'

Irene smiled and there was in her smile a slight hint of embarrassment, as if mention of her secondary school had stirred uncomfortable memories.

Wendell suddenly felt excluded. He sensed that the years separating Irene and Stevie were not as many as the years separating him and Irene.

Victor Barrett, famous in school for his football skills, now joined the group and engaged Stevie Johnson in chat.

Wendell, pleased to have Irene's full attention again, felt compelled to compliment her on her appearance. 'You look fantastic, Irene. Hard to believe you're a grandmother.'

'Thank you,' she said, 'but you haven't seen the hard work that goes into being me.'

They laughed together and Wendell experienced a brief flashback of playing with the skinny girl in the stairwell of the house where she lived. And the memory made him wonder how she had been able to lure him there over so many evenings. Or had he lured her? And when her brother invited him to listen to music and played Led Zeppelin's 'Whole Lotta Love', had Dion known about their regular after-school dates in the stairwell?

Stevie and Victor now rejoined them and Wendell welcomed their return because in the few minutes he had spent with Irene too many memories and questions had formed in his mind.

Wendell spent the rest of the night moving between small groups of old schoolfriends. Pictures were taken on mobile phones, numbers were exchanged and there was much talk of a school reunion later in the year, after the funeral and reception for Dion.

As the Nine Night was drawing to a close, Wendell stood with a group of men in the foyer of the building.

Irene passed them and said goodbye, and Stevie Johnson broke away from the group and walked out into the car park with her. Wendell's back stiffened; he had intuited a familiarity between them. He felt a searing pain in his chest and took a step back, to lean against the wall.

That was when he overheard Victor Barrett say to Trevor Haynes: 'Looks as if Stevie is still sweet on Irene.'

'Still sweet?'

'Yeah, man. Those two go way, way back. Used to meet on Paddington Green at lunchtime. Saw each other for years after school.'

Wendell's pain subsided and he began to doubt his memory of the events from school. Is that what the fight with Stevie Johnson had been about? No. Stevie Johnson was always fighting with other boys and it had been Wendell's turn on that day. When and why had he stopped seeing Irene? he asked himself. Was it before or after she and Stevie started meeting on the Green? Had she been seeing them both at the same time, one at lunchtime, the other after school? He had no answers to these questions, which swirled around in his mind with a growing feeling of foolishness.

By the time he got home that night Wendell felt a lot lighter and smiled at his own romantic view of the past in which Irene was his first true love. A delusion had been punctured, and he felt that maybe this was the gift of reaching a certain age, a clearer picture of reality, despite unreliable memories of the distant past.

He was still mulling over the Nine Night a few evenings later, in between reading a great nineteenth-century Russian novel, when he received a call from an unknown number. He answered it.

'Wendell Clarke?'

'Yes.'

'It's Stevie Johnson here. Got your number from Trevor.'

'OK.'

'How you doing, sir?'

'I am fine. And you?'

'I'm cool. Just wanted to say it was good seeing you again, sir.'

'It was good seeing you, too. But why are you calling me "sir"?'

'Being humble, ain't I.'

'Oh, then I should be calling you "sir", also. We were in the same school, the same year, even the same house. "Sir".'

Stevie laughed and said, 'When I was young I loved fighting, I was always picking fights with other guys. Then when I was around twenty-one, I discovered martial arts – you know, karate and kung fu. You probably did, too.'

'Liked some of the movies, but I have never practised any martial arts.'

'Anyway, that's how I stopped picking fights.'

Wendell understood that Stevie Johnson was offering an explanation, and maybe the closest he would ever come to making an apology, for the school playground fight of over fifty years before. Again he remembered the day when, enraged and confused, he had stumbled into the library and found peace in its silence. And he looked at the wall of books in the room where he sat and thought of the fantastic journeys he had made through the humanities and social sciences; the popular science books that had given him an understanding of astronomy and palaeontology; his awareness of his own vast ignorance, with each snippet of knowledge he gained; the plays he had seen; the dance performances he had watched; the art galleries and exhibitions he had visited; the poems and novels he had read and planned to read. Maybe he would have made those journeys anyway, without encountering Stevie Johnson, but he saw no harm in acknowledging Stevie's contribution, whatever its weight.

He said: 'Thank you, Stevie, thank you very much. I am grateful.'

'What for?'

He hesitated for a second and decided it would be impossible to explain the reason for his gratitude. He settled for saying, 'For calling. Thanks for calling, yeah.'

'Could we keep in touch?'

'Sure. That would be nice.'

They said their goodbyes. Wendell put the phone aside and took a sip of water. Then he picked up the epic Russian novel and was soon immersed in it again, its words and sentences transporting him to another country and another time.

Please Knock and Wait

The front door banged shut and the sound reverberated through the house and penetrated Karl's sleep. He pulled the blanket over his head, but when he imagined hearing his father's loud, harsh voice saying, 'Get up and get on with the day,' he knew the night was over. Expelled from sleep, eyes still shut, and buried beneath the blanket, he thought of Sophia and wondered whether she would be waiting for him on Edgware Road, in the doorway between the photography studio and the Oriental carpet shop. He could see them walking together as far as the tube station, where they would part to head off to their respective schools, she to the girls' school opposite Paddington Green, and he to the boys' school behind the Bakerloo line tube station.

He pushed aside the blanket, got out of bed and dressed in the cold, dark room.

Ten minutes later, schoolbag on his lap, he sat in a front seat on the upper deck of the number 36 as it sped through the retreating night. Frost shimmered on roofs and cars, house lights blinked on and off, steam curled from open windows; a passing milk float made a musical noise. The upper deck remained half empty until the bus reached Harrow Road, where it suddenly filled up.

The passengers were mostly men. A large brown-skinned man slumped beside Karl and muttered something incomprehensible and weary-sounding as he dropped his canvas tool bag on the floor. Karl sat upright to make more space on the seat and, using the back of his hand, wiped the steamed-up window, creating a round viewing area like a ship's porthole.

The bus was driving eastward. At the cast-iron bridge over the Grand Union Canal, Harrow Road plunged – and for an instant the landscape seemed to open up. It was Karl's favourite moment in the journey, this point where the Westway flyover curved through the darkness like a grey serpent, and rectangular-shaped tower blocks rose from the sprawling Warwick housing estate; and in the distance, he knew, the city continued for miles and miles to the river and beyond.

When the bus reached the bottom of the incline, as if burrowing into the land, his thoughts turned to Sophia again. They had met at the joint Christmas Party held for sixth-formers from Rutherford and Sarah Siddons School. They had never dated formally, he did not even have her telephone number. The previous Friday, crossing Sussex Gardens, she had allowed him to hold her slender, bony hand. But the following Monday, at the same junction, when he tried to repeat the act, she had pulled her hand away, leaving him grasping air. It was as though the intervening weekend had destroyed their intimacy, and he was worried that it would be weeks before he could again take her hand.

The sight of Paddington station ended his reverie. The pull of the city became stronger from here and he followed the bus's progress down Praed Street, watched it turn south as it edged onto a busy Edgware Road, and felt a slight thrill as some minutes later it swept round Marble Arch. A feeble grey daylight had arrived by the time he disembarked on Park Lane.

He entered the brightly lit lobby of the Norfolk Hotel through the side door and went to the Apollo kiosk, which sold tobacco, confectionary and newspapers. Rachel was already there. Plump, with brown cropped hair and large green eyes, she was a trainee teacher at a primary school in Pimlico.

'Good morning, Karl. I see you managed to arrive on time this morning.' She glanced at her watch and added, 'In fact, you're a whole ten minutes early.'

'I haven't been late for weeks,' Karl said.

A month after starting this job, he had overslept and arrived thirty minutes late, and though he had been punctual since that calamitous morning, Rachel often teased him about his timekeeping.

'Have to keep you on your toes, Karl; you know that. It is a truth universally acknowledged that boys are innately lazy, if only because being a girl is hard work, hard work best started early in the morning. It's my divine duty to rid you of your laziness.'

'You and my father should meet one day,' Karl said. He went behind the kiosk and put down his school bag.

Rachel smiled and her large eyes sparkled, and Karl was reminded of a furry nocturnal creature. She pointed to a pile of already marked newspapers.

'It's a small round today. Shouldn't take long. Oh, and there's a PKW among them.'

He looked at her blankly.

'Please knock and wait. Really Karl, you should know that by now.'

'Oh, yes,' Karl muttered, thinking he would hate to be one of Rachel's pupils. PKWs were rare.

He started on the top floor and worked his way down, dropping the newspapers on the thick carpet outside the doors in the narrow, dimly lit corridors. Only a few papers remained when he arrived at the PKW marked on *The Times*. He was on the second floor. To his surprise, the door was ajar and there was a vague smell of soap and a trace of steam. He knocked firmly and the sound seemed to reverberate down the corridor.

'Come in,' a male voice returned.

Karl pushed the door further open and stepped into a square, high-ceilinged lobby area. The smell of soap was stronger here.

'Just give me a moment.'

He looked to his left and saw, standing in a doorway of swirling steam, a man towelling himself down. He had an even, matt black complexion, and the large white towel and steam combined to create a near-spectral effect. His hair was wavy, almost straight, and some of it was plastered to his forehead. His nipples were a different colour from his body, his stomach was flat but not muscular and his torso tapered to a narrow waist. His penis was a broad stubby thing; limp, it nestled on his scrotum in a bed of wiry hair. His legs, like his chest, were covered in the same black wavy hair.

Karl was no stranger to naked male bodies; the shower room after school football matches teemed with them. And of course he had often scrutinised reflections of his own naked body in the mirror of the Edwardian wardrobe in his bedroom. But he could not recall ever having seen a mature naked male body, and like the bus crossing the Grand Union Canal, it was, for an instant, an arresting sight that stirred an indefinable feeling in him.

The man gave Karl a brilliant white smile and said, 'Take it to the room, please.'

Karl stepped into the bedroom and waited. The red and green curtains were slightly parted and he could see the winter-dead trees across Park Lane, in Hyde Park. The bed was unkempt and the light from a bedside lamp fell onto the white sheets and pillows. Karl placed the paper on the varnished surface of a sideboard.

Less than a minute later the guest entered the room. He was now swaddled in a white towelling bathrobe. He brushed past Karl, picked up the newspaper, and went to stand with his back to the window.

'That was good timing,' he said. 'Any earlier and I wouldn't have heard you.'

As Karl tried to formulate a reply, he thought he recognised a familiar rhythm to the man's accent.

'Hope I didn't embarrass you,' the man said.

'No, sir.'

'Good. Now wait a minute. Where did I put my wallet?'

Karl finally recognised the man's accent. It was Jamaican, softer, less guttural than his father's but unmistakably Jamaican.

The man threw the newspaper on the unmade bed and went to the bedside table.

'Are you Jamaican?' Karl asked.

'Yes, for my sins. And you, you're a black Englishman, I take it?'

Karl was puzzled. The combination of black and Englishman seemed odd, almost oxymoronic.

'Not quite,' he replied. 'I was born in Jamaica. Been here since I was five.'

'Oh, really. Now that's interesting. Name's Orson Carter. And yours?'

'Karl Riverson.'

'Riverson. I know one or two Riversons. Where on the island are your parents from?'

Karl hesitated. He did not want to reveal that his parents were separated, and that he did not know exactly where they came from on the island. 'Kingston,' he answered. 'Least, that's where I was born.'

'It's possible they were born in Kingston. But most people in Kingston come from somewhere else. You should make sure. Ask them. How long have you been working for the hotel?

'I don't work for the hotel. I work for Apollo, the kiosk in the lobby. I'm still at school. The sixth form.'

'Ah, a studious young man. Good for you. We need young men like you in Jamaica. Take a seat.' He nodded at an armchair, and Karl perched on one of its arms.

'You don't sound much like a Jamaican,' Karl said, looking at the man as though he were some strange and fabulous creature. A Jamaican in the Norfolk Hotel. He could not wait to tell his friends and his father.

'You mean I don't say rass and rawtid. I can if you want. If it makes you feel more comfortable.' The man laughed and threw his head back as though he were pleased with his own sense of humour. He revealed that he worked for a consortium of Caribbean distilleries and he was part of a marketing delegation touring Europe to promote rum; he was scheduled to fly to France later in the day.

Karl liked his soft, even voice, his gentle manners and easy laugh. All the adult Jamaican men he knew were loud, tough men, like his father. He told Orson of his ambitions to attend university, though he didn't know what he wanted to study as yet. Then an image of Sophia standing in the doorway between the shop that sold Oriental carpets and the photography studio flashed in Karl's mind and he became conscious of the time. He stood up and said he had to leave.

'Well, good meeting you,' Orson Carter said, rising from the bed. 'Ah, just remembered. I don't have any sterling. But what I can give you is this.' He walked past Karl, opened the sideboard and pulled out an earthenware flagon of rum. He handed it to Karl, saying, 'Give this to your father. Jamaican dark rum. The best.'

Karl took the flagon and though his father was not a drinker, he knew it would impress him.

'And here's my card. Look me up when you're in Jamaica.'

They parted at the door with a firm handshake, and Karl proceeded to finish his newspaper round feeling somehow different because he had never really considered himself anything but Karl Riverson, a sixth-former, and within the space of minutes somebody had called him a black Englishman and a Jamaican, and he had never given much thought to being either a black Englishman or a Jamaican, so there was a lot to think about.

Karl delivered the other newspapers and returned to the kiosk. Rachel expressed surprise that he had taken so long and congratulated him for receiving such a wonderful gift. 'Make sure you do take it home to your father,' she said.

'Of course I will,' Karl replied.

He said goodbye and dashed outside into Park Lane, which was streaming with traffic. Fearing that he would be late, he wondered whether he should take a bus, but decided that as he would have to cross the busy road it would be just as quick to walk. With his schoolbag feeling heavy, he reached the shop doorway on Edgware Road and saw that it was empty. His watch told him he was on time; he had arrived later than this and found Sophia waiting.

As he stood there, an image of Orson Carter naked and dripping with water came to his memory. Again he was struck by the beauty and mystery of Orson's naked body. Then the thought that he might be queer disturbed him and brought another memory to the forefront of his consciousness. It had happened at primary school. Sport days involved an hour-long coach journey to reach playing fields on the edge of London. On one such trip, he was seated next to John Harrison, a small blond boy. They started playing Pitty-Patt and some point John began showering Karl with kisses. Karl resisted playfully. The same thing happened again the following week. Soon he was looking forward to playing with John. Standing in the doorway between the Oriental carpet shop and photography studio, he could not recall when or why he stopped playing with John Harrison, and this hiatus in his memory worried him.

'Hello, Karl.'

He looked and saw Sophia. She was wearing a black knee-length coat and her long, straight dark hair rested on her shoulders. Her narrow face was powdered white, as usual.

'Hello, Sophia,' he said, smiling.

'You seemed to be a million miles away.'

'I was just trying to remember something from my past.'

He stepped out of the doorway, and with the rush-hour traffic roaring and coughing and horns blowing, they strolled towards their schools further down Edgware Road. Karl's school bag touched Sophia, alerting her to the bulge caused by the flagon of rum, and she asked what he was carrying. He gave her a much-edited account of his encounter with the Jamaican in the Norfolk Hotel.

'Lucky you,' she said.

At Sussex Gardens they had to wait for the lights to change. Karl shifted his bag onto his right shoulder. The lights changed, they stepped into the road and he reached for Sophia's hand and found it ready and open to receive his own hand. But halfway across the road, this public declaration of their affection for each other, this gesture he had been looking forward to since waking up, seemed to be both uncomfortable and inexplicably wrong, and he obeyed an overpowering need to release her hand.

Christmas Fire

Christmas was approaching and London glittered and sparkled with seasonal decorations, and songs and carols could be heard everywhere. That Saturday, Clive Stewart was walking along Morning Lane in Hackney when he spotted a shop selling coal-effect electric fires with an ersatz wooden surround. They were advertised by a large colour poster of a family – parents and two rosy-cheeked children – gathered round a fireplace with a glowing flame, and next to them was a Christmas tree under which sat a pile of presents that had been wrapped with great artistry. The words read: *Give your family a perfect Christmas.* Clive Stewart decided on the spot to do just that. Such a purchase would delight his wife and thrill their two children.

He strode into the shop, made enquiries from a smooth-talking, unctuous salesman, who assured him that it would take a competent handyman less than a day to install the whole thing and recreate in his home a centrepiece for an unforgettable festive occasion. Clive was more than a handyman, he was a builder who had once owned his own company. So he went to a nearby hardware store and bought a wheelbarrow – an item he had been wanting for some time – placed the boxed fire in it, wished the salesman a very Merry Christmas, and left the shop feeling pleased with himself.

Pushing the wheelbarrow containing the large box along the crowded pavement of Saturday shoppers, Clive was a picture of happiness. He whistled and greeted strangers like a man on Prozac. In this buoyant mood, the journey to his home in Stoke Newington posed no threat. He was still under forty years of age and worked out at the gym three times a week; he looked remarkably fit, though a little neglectful of his clothing.

Near a junction on Mare Street, Clive saw a young woman squatting in a disused shop doorway. Hands outstretched, she was one of the many beggars who daily descended on this shopping area in its busiest hours. He was struck by her youth, her large eyes and ashen complexion, and saddened by the means by which she had been forced to live. He stopped, searched his pockets for some loose change, and as he was about to give her some coins, it occurred to him that he could be far more generous: he would invite her home, provide her with warmth, shelter and the friendship of his family for the festive season.

Clive beamed his warmest smile at the young woman as he extended his invitation. She frowned with suspicion. But when he showed her the photograph of his wife and children that he always carried in his wallet, and told her she would have her own bedroom with a lock and key and hot baths whenever she liked, her suspicion gave way to belief and trust and she accepted his invitation.

Her name was Hilary. She was wore thick striped leggings, a man's grey overcoat and green boots with multi-coloured laces.

Pushing the wheelbarrow and accompanied by Hilary, Clive set off for home. They talked as they walked.

'What's in the box?' Hilary asked.

'It's an electric coal-effect fire, with the surrounds, everything. Going to install it myself, give my family a perfect Christmas.'

'I can't remember when I last spent Christmas with my family,' Hilary said, sounding much older than she looked. She told Clive about Christmases at home in Leeds and the fireplace with the cast-iron coal fire, slate hearth and oak surround. The memory seemed to cheer her up and there was a visible spring in her step.

'Well, this will be just as good, probably better,' Clive said. 'We won't be able to roast chestnuts or marshmallows, but my wife bakes a great black cake. That's what we Jamaicans eat instead of Christmas pudding. She's been soaking the currants and raisins in rum since September. When you taste this cake, you won't want to touch another Christmas pudding.' Clive laughed heartily. A five-week holiday in Jamaica many years before was his only experience of the island, but he took great pride in asserting his Jamaican-ness.

Every so often, Clive stopped to rest. He would breathe in deeply and stretch his muscles. His arms were aching now but he was used to physical exertion. Picking up the handles of the wheelbarrow, he said: 'That's the problem with modern life. Not enough exercise. When I was younger I was an ace football player, a champion middle-distance runner. You've got to keep in shape.'

Hilary nodded, stomped her feet and hugged herself in a gesture intended to keep herself warm, but which betrayed a feeling of ineffable loneliness.

Some yards after that stop, Clive turned onto Graham Road and, passing Harry Bovell's house, he heard music and figured that Harry, a frequent party-giver, was having a gathering. They were halfway home, so Clive decided that this would be a good point to take a proper rest before continuing the journey. He pushed the wheelbarrow into the garden, then went to press the doorbell.

Harry Bovell answered the door. He was a small, stout, jolly-looking man. He appeared surprised to see Clive but greeted him with practised warmth.

'Clive, long time, man, How you doing? I've been meaning to look you up, but you know how Christmas is. Family first, eh? What's that you got in the wheelbarrow?'

'It's an electric fire, coal-effect, plus surrounds. I'm going to give Ann and the kids a perfect Christmas.'

Harry Bovell cleared his throat, scratched his head and looked quizzically at Clive.

'Yes, man. Perfect Christmas,' Clive repeated.

'Come in,' Harry said.

'Okay. But can't stop for long. And this is Hilary.'

Harry greeted Hilary and Hilary greeted Harry.

'She's going to spend Christmas with my family, aren't you, Hilary?'

'Yes, yes,' Hilary said.

Several guests, men and women, were in the long narrow room and they were sipping rum. A football game was in progress on the giant colour television screen. Clive and Hilary were introduced. Hilary accepted a glass of wine from Harry's wife, Babsy. Clive refused alcohol, settling for water, and proceeded to make small talk with Harry's friends, some of whom he knew.

One of the guests was Ronnie Blake and he said to Clive, 'Still working on the house?'

'No, no, finished long time now. Put on a new roof, replaced most of the joists, re-plastered all the walls. You know these old Victorian houses, got to take care of them. Took me years though. Used to come home from work and get stuck in, worked into the night. But it's worth it. You must come over at Christmas. Taste some of Ann's black cake.'

'Sure, sure,' Ronnie Blake said, moving away abruptly from Clive to speak to someone else.

Clive was not fond of Ronnie Blake. They had once quarrelled, and he regretted having invited him to drop in at Christmas because while he couldn't remember exactly what they had quarrelled about, he was sure there was still some enmity between them, otherwise why had the other man ended their exchange so suddenly? Clive mused on broken friendships for a moment then fell into conversation with another guest.

Hilary was having a good time. She aroused curiosity in this gathering of Caribbean folks and Babsy, Harry's wife, was fussing over her. But mindful of the journey ahead, Clive pulled her aside and reminded her that they still had some distance to go, and should leave now as he wanted to get home before dark and make a start on installing the fire that would give his family, and her, a perfect Christmas.

So they set off again. When Clive found himself pushing the wheelbarrow through a crowded Ridley Road market, he regretted not taking a longer route around it. Emerging from the market, he spotted Vera Bolton, and as he had not seen her in ages and was a little tired, he stopped. He was sure they had once been good friends, but couldn't remember exactly when. Vera greeted Clive with chilling formality.

'What's with the wheelbarrow?' she asked rather scornfully.

'It's a fire, an electric fire – coal effect. Mock wood surround. Going to give my family a perfect Christmas.'

'Better than the one you gave me two Christmases ago,' Vera said, sniffing the air and glancing at Hilary.

Clive suddenly remembered. 'Oh, that's such a long time ago. You know I couldn't help it. Ann wouldn't let me out of her sights.'

'You could've called,' Vera said. 'I waited and waited and eventually drank myself to sleep. You bastard.'

Her voice had risen and Clive glanced around embarrassedly, while Hilary looked on, puzzled.

'Look, I am sorry, Vera. I really am. Can't you forget it?'

'No, Clive, no,' Vera said, brushing past him. 'In future when you see me on the street, don't talk to me, because I won't see you.'

Vera hurried away, and Clive watched her for a moment before picking up the wheelbarrow and moving on. He walked faster now and Hilary had to make an effort to keep up with him.

Five minutes later, approaching the Caribbean Joint Restaurant and Take-away, where three men stood outside chewing the rag, Clive tried to hurry past. But he overheard one of the men say: 'Isn't that Clive Stewart? Heard he was having some family troubles. Looks like he found himself a new wife.' And they all laughed meanly and lasciviously.

Clive stopped, left his wheelbarrow and Hilary, walked back to the men and gave them a good piece of his mind, which alluded to their laziness, worthlessness and habit of spreading nasty rumours. A fight would have broken out if one of the men had not acted as a peacemaker and urged Clive to continue on his way.

Clive returned to the wheelbarrow and Hilary in a state of extreme agitation, cursing the men.

Hilary now seemed uncomfortable. She said: 'I don't think I want to come home with you any longer.'

'Don't be silly,' Clive said earnestly. 'It will be a perfect Christmas. You'll be in a family. We'll treat you just like one of the family. You'll even get a present and everything. And when you taste my wife's cake ...' He rolled his eyes to suggest a delicious, even heavenly taste.

'No, no', Hilary said, shaking her head and backing away from Clive as if suddenly frightened of something in his voice. 'I'm not going anywhere with you.'

Clive stood and watched as she hurried away. He wondered briefly how she would spend Christmas and decided, with a measure of disappointment and resignation, that some people just can't be rescued from their wretched state. Then he picked up the handles of his wheelbarrow and moved on.

His mood improved as he pushed the wheelbarrow containing the box with the electric coal-effect fire. He recalled hearing on the radio a weather forecast predicting snow on Christmas Day. The prospect of a white Christmas cheered him even further. If it did snow, he would make a snowman with the children in the back garden, a snowman with a carrot nose and potato eyes and wearing an old hat. As if in response to this thought, the sky spat a few snowflakes, and he whistled as he pushed the wheelbarrow.

Finally he reached the street where he lived. The thin rowan trees were bare of leaves and, with a few exceptions, the two-storey terraced houses, like everywhere he had passed, showed signs of the festive season. There were Christmas trees in the windows, some ablaze with electric lights, mistletoe dangling, and he could see holly wreaths attached to front doors.

He was sweating as he approached his own house and felt relieved as he pushed the wheelbarrow through the gate, which made a loud creaking noise. He opened the front door, lifted the box out of the wheelbarrow and entered the house with it. He stepped on to a pile of unopened letters, placed the box down on the floor and wondered why the children had not run to greet him. Then he glanced at the shadows on the walls where pictures had once hung, and when the silence and desolation in the house struck him like a cold blast of air, he remembered.

Dawg Dead

His name was Dawg and for over ten years, until the day that wild animal attacked and killed him, he was truly my good, good friend, my best friend. I'm telling you, he was a good friend. The best. Truly! And if there was any justice in this world, and I mean justice, not a whole heap of cockamamy laws devised by madmen, enforced by crooks and practised by conmen, if there was any justice in this world, Dawg's killer would not be walking the streets today, free, free. It pain me to know that Dawg's killer still walking free. It pain me, it pain me, it pain me, you see.

Me and Dawg used to go for some long, long walks. Some long walks, yeah. Ain't a park in London that me and Dawg ain't walk through. Hyde Park, Regent's Park, St James's Park, Hampstead Heath, Alexandra Palace, Hackney Marshes, Epsom Forest – yes, me and Dawg been to all them places. Even took a day trip to Brighton once. Should have seen Dawg swimming in the sea. What a sight! What a sight! Mostly though we walked in our local park, Clissold Park. We walk in that park through rain. We walk through snow. We walk through hailstones big like marbles. I knew every tree and bench where Dawg left his scent: the third bench on the Green Lanes side, the second horse chestnut tree on that same side, the plane tree near the lake ... could go on and on.

Yes, me and Dawg did some walking in our time. And he never complained. You see, that is one of the things I used to love about Dawg. He never complained. Never complained. Even that last morning, when he looked kinda tired and was moving slower than the rush-hour traffic, as soon as he saw the leash in my hand, he waddled to the front door, his belly almost touching the floor. Never complained. What a friend! And he made me some good friends, too. Like Chris. He's moved away now, gone back home to Cumbria. Still sends me a card every Christmas. Met him in Clissold Park when Dawg and his dog, a German Shepherd, pure, called Latch – funny name to give a dog – got friendly. First time they met they chased each other in circles for a full ten minutes before we could get them under control. Me and Chris just watched and laughed.

'Looks like your dog has quite a bit of Alsatian in him,' Chris said.

'And some Collie and Labrador,' I said. 'Least that's what they told me when I got him from Battersea Dogs' Home.'

'Latch is a thoroughbred,' Chris said.

I knew later that he didn't mean to sound superior or boastful about his dog, but he did – just the way some white people speak – so I replied in my own superior tone, which I knew how to turn on because I'd spent many years in the welding business as a sub-contractor. You see – and I know I'm digressing here, but I'll get back to me and Chris in a moment – you see, I came here with a few years' experience as a welder and walked straight into a job. One day, the foreman said to me, 'What does it feel like, being the only black person working here?' I looked at him for a while, then looked around at my workmates – did everything real slow – then looked back at him and said, 'You know, I didn't notice until you pointed it out.'

So anyway, I said to Chris, 'Well, you see, Dawg is like me. A mongrel.'

'You're a mongrel?'

'I mean mixed, mixed. From the West Indies, you see. Father from Panama. Never knew him. Mother from Jamaica. On her side, a few generations back there was a Scot, and further back a Portuguese Jew, and even further back some Africans. Can't say exactly where they came from though, the Africans, I mean.'

'Oh, I see. Sadly, I'm just an Englishman.'

'You mean you ain't got no Scottish, Irish or Welsh blood in you? Not a drop?'

'Far as I know.'

'That's something else,' I said, thinking how on a small piece of land like this anybody could claim pure blood – also hearing in Chris's voice the tones of an educated man.

I went on, 'Been here since I was sixteen and now I'm over sixty and I ain't never met a thoroughbred Englishman. Ain't that something! Oh well, ain't nothing to be ashamed of, being a pure-blooded Englishman.'

'That's very kind of you. Very kind.'

We laughed and that was when I really noticed Chris, hearing that deep, roaring laugh and thinking, If a man can laugh like that, I mean really surrender himself to laughter for an instant, he must be an all-right sort of a man. Now, I ain't saying that you can tell everything about a person by his laugh, but you can tell quite a bit – more than his eyes, which is where some people say you tells a man's soul from, but I don't agree – don't even know what a soul is, if you really want to know the truth.

Anyway, before I turn down another side road, that was how me and Chris became friends. Because our dogs became friends. Would never pass each other in the park without stopping for a chat while our dogs romped. Met his wife, his three children. Even had dinner with them one Christmas. Lovely people.

Yes, Dawg was my best friend and through him I met some good people. Some very good people.

Take Lisa. Dawg must have been about three years old when I met her. She had a little Jack Russell, called him JR. Man, that dog was as bright as the pole star. Swear he understood every word we said, and probably understood French, Italian and German, maybe even Mandarin. And he walked with a swagger that said he believed he was the brightest dog to ever set foot in the park. Dawg and JR became great friends. See, he saw something in Dawg, something beyond all that mess of hair and sleepy eyes like a fool's, something that I'd recognised straight away: intelligence.

As for Lisa, we became more than friends. Let me tell you about Lisa ... no, I can't tell you about Lisa. Not yet. The memories are too sweet, too sweet to share. All I'll say is that I should have met her when I was a younger man, would have got down on my knees and begged her to marry me, maybe taken her back to Jamaica, built a hillside house for her with a view of the sea on one side and a view of the mountains on the other side, and a purple bougainvillea hedge surrounding the land; or moved to Kent or some such place, buy a nice little cottage for us there, place with a view of green fields, rolling hills, misty mornings.

Yes, that woman made me dream again, but I was already getting on in age then, and when you're above a certain age, ain't no point in dreaming too hard, dreaming till you sweat, unless you looking for an early grave. Because you ain't got the energy to make that dream come true, only enough energy to take your dog for a daily walk round the park, and stroll around your mind among all the stupid things you did in your youth, like always wanting to get under a woman's skirt when the real prize is in her heart and mind, but you're too young and stupid to recognise that.

Yes, man, Lisa made me dream again for a while and for that alone, I have to thank her, as well as for the conversations on the park bench under clear summer skies, or on nippy autumn days when all the leaves have turned gold and conkers and acorns are strewn on the grass, signs that winter ain't far away but you're not worried because you have Dawg, and Lisa is in your life, and just to sit beside her on a park bench, or stroll for a while, and talk about this and that was warmth enough for the coldest winter day. The coldest. And without Dawg, I wouldn't have met her. She moved to Portugal a few years back, and some days I miss her so I could cry. But I ain't going to tell you more than that about Lisa.

Now Dawg's gone, too. Cried a few times. I tried telling the judge some of that, what I lost when that wild animal killed my dog, Dawg, but he didn't want to know. Should have got myself a lawyer, he told me. A lawyer? Would have had to mortgage my house to get one. Besides, the police told me I had a strong case. That wild animal should have been on a leash, minimum. Had a history of attacking other dogs. And that morning when he went for Dawg, the poor thing didn't stand a chance. He was too old to fight back, too old. That wild animal should have been put down.

Poor Dawg. He's dead, dead, dead. Killed. His throat ripped open by a wild animal on a bright spring morning. And I couldn't get no justice for Dawg. No justice for Dawg. It make me want to bawl, that I couldn't get no justice for Dawg.

The Beautiful Laundress

From behind the counter she watched as Martin bundled the half-dry clothes into a plastic bag. She was tempted to intervene and offer him, a regular customer, more drying time, free of charge, but kept quiet because she didn't want him to think her heart had softened. Some months before, at an hour when the launderette was empty, he, a widower, had declared his affection for her and she had, with some delicacy, spurned him, telling him in her halting English that he had misunderstood her friendliness. It was her business to help customers and make them feel comfortable in the launderette. Since then the easy exchanges between them had stopped and now he, a man scorned, barely looked at her. She watched him zip up the bag. 'Bye, Olga,' he said and left.

Later that February morning, after the first wave of customers, Olga was gazing out at the street from within the launderette, beyond the silent washers and dryers, sparkling as if they had just left the factory. Olga took great pride in her work. Her service washes were always returned neatly folded, and her skill at repairing torn dresses, blouses and trousers had earned her many customers by word of mouth.

As she looked out at the street she thought of her former home in Lithuania, the house with enough land around it for a large barn where they kept chickens and pigs: her soldier-father had built it, freeing her and her mother from the long, endless queues. She remembered, too, the flight to Switzerland after perestroika to escape her violent husband, working as a seamstress in a Zurich shop that sold wedding dresses, then being tempted to London by a compatriot who promised her love and then abandoned her in a Tottenham bedsit. And when she remembered all the upheavals and journeys, it seemed to Olga that she had had a hard life, but she had made a fresh start in London. The city had dressed her in an entirely new outfit called freedom, freedom from what she, a woman in her mid-forties, now recognised as the false hopes of youth. Love? Marriage? Property and money in the bank were all that interested her now.

The sudden dimming of the light in the doorway registered on her consciousness before she saw the customer enter. He was a middle-aged man, clean-shaven and dark, and wearing a navy-blue fleece speckled with white and green paint, a green cotton polo-neck top, blue tracksuit bottoms and white trainers. He carried a black plastic bag. She had been doing the job long enough to recognise all her regular customers. He was a stranger.

The man walked up to the counter, heaved the bag on to it, exhaled loudly and said, 'Good morning, madam, I need a service wash.' His formal address took her aback for a second and when she recovered, she explained the prices, felt the bag and told him it was a large wash. She then opened the bag and saw that it was all bedlinen.

'That's fine,' he said. 'When can I pick it up?'

She glanced at the clock and said, 'Come at four o'clock.'

'Five o'clock would be best for me,' he said.

She took out her service-wash book, filled in the relevant section, and asked him his name.

'Williams,' he said.

Her written English always failed her and she asked him to spell out the name. Then she said, 'Pay now or later?'

'Later.'

She handed him the ticket and he took it and said, 'Thank you, madam. I look forward to sleeping on clean sheets. My washing machine has broken down.'

'Oh, sorry,' she said.

'And I didn't renew the repair warranty. False economy. Now I have to find the funds to buy a new machine.'

'These modern machines! Not good.'

'Maybe. Anyway, once again, thank you, madam. You shall see me at or around five p.m.'

She watched him leave and thought he could do with losing some weight; she also tried to recall the last time she had been called madam three times within the space of ten minutes, and decided that 'madam' suited her at this stage in her life.

As she emptied the bag into one of the bigger washing machines, Olga noticed that all the pillowcases and bedsheets were made of pure cotton, with one sheet of brushed cotton, which had a luxurious feel. She was used to washing polyester and other man-made fabrics but she knew good cloth just by touching it. She wondered who the owner was, with his formal manners, and imagined that he lived in a house, unlike most of her customers who came from the surrounding housing estates.

Pity he's black, she thought, and was instantly ashamed of this thought because though she had never had a black lover she had lived long enough away from home to know that colour was only skin-deep. How many times had she been arrested by the sight of some African woman wearing a flamboyantly coloured dress that served to heighten her matt black skin, or some besuited tall smooth dark man with symmetrical features and an attractively lazy walk that suggested someone who was used to walking long distances under a scorching sun? But she most regretted the thought, 'Pity he's black,' because it betrayed a desire based on what the man owned, and she could never desire a man for that reason alone. In fact, why the hell was she even thinking about a man! Those days were over. She owned her flat in London and another in Lithuania, and the most she could realistically look forward to now was a peaceful and comfortable retirement.

There was a steady stream of customers over the next few hours, all regulars who needed no help with operating the machines so Olga could concentrate on her repair work and service washes. Early in the afternoon there was a lull for fifteen minutes when the launderette was empty. It ended with the arrival of her friend Mercedes, a Sicilian, who came in to use a dryer and they spent some time trading gossip. Not that Olga had much gossip to give in exchange for Mercedes's relentless flow of stories about the people where she lived. Mercedes's latest news was that her Portuguese neighbour had driven her husband away, back to Lisbon, because she had her sights set on a recently retired schoolteacher originally from Cameroon. 'Imagine that,' Mercedes said. 'Her husband – and for an African.'

Remembering her own shameful thought, Olga said, 'You think it wouldn't be so bad if it was for a white man?'

'No. All bad. A wife belongs with her husband, till death.'

Olga liked Mercedes in part because they both shared the Catholic faith, but while Olga wore her religion lightly, it seemed to her that Mercedes's Catholicism was a heavy dark shawl that made her movements rigid, inflexible. She, Olga, had been married at nineteen, in the church, but not even the pope could have prevented her from fleeing, six years later, her foulmouthed and violent husband. Mercedes, Olga decided, had been lucky. Her husband was soft-spoken, simple and kind.

An hour after Mercedes had left, Mr Williams returned for his laundry. He paid, thanked Olga again with his formal manners, took the bagged bed linen and bade her goodbye. He walked towards the door, then turned back, smiled and said to her: 'I think you're rather beautiful, madam. Where are you from?'

'Thank you,' she said, feeling herself blush. 'Lithuania.'

'Oh, that sounds far, far north. A cold country?'

'Not all the time. We have a summer. And you, where are you from?'

'It's very complicated. But let's just say Jamaica, the tropics.'

'It's warm, yes?'

'Very warm. You must visit it sometime. I must go. I look forward to sleeping on these clean sheets folded by your fair hands.' Then he was gone.

Spring came early that year and Olga had forgotten about the Jamaican until he reappeared in mid-April. He wore blue cotton trousers, a faded linen jacket, and a pair of brown brogues. He had grown a goatee beard. He thanked her for having rescued him during the depth of winter when his washing machine, now fixed, had failed him, and presented her with a gift.

She held the green object in her hand, and said, 'What is it?'

'You don't know what this is?'

'No.'

'It's a mango, of course.'

'Oh, a mango. I've seen them on television, but not like this.'

'Ah, that's because this is a Julie mango. Leave it in your fruit bowl for a few days, maybe till Sunday.'

Olga was reminded of the sharp sweet taste of the mango when, a week later, the Jamaican came into the launderette again.

'How was the mango, madam?'

'It was delicious,' she smiled.

'I hope it was as delicious as you are beautiful, madam.'

She erupted in laughter and noticed for the first time the playful sparkle in his eyes.

'That's not for me to say,' she said.

Over the next few months, the Jamaican visited the launderette almost weekly, always bringing her a different gift: papaya (with some limes), sarsaparilla, custard apple, passion fruit, Bombay, Honey and East Indian mangoes, soursop (with a whole nutmeg and vanilla pods and instructions on how to make a drink out of the pimply fruit), and a slice of jackfruit. He was always in a hurry, so said very little, and once when she accepted his gift and laughed, saying, 'You spoil me,' he replied in earnest, 'Madam, if Lithuania was careless enough to let you leave, then we here in London must show our appreciation of your beauty and ensure that you never return.'

She did not understand everything he had said, but she caught the gist of it and his words sounded as sweet as papaya with a squeeze of lime juice on a Sunday morning.

The next time she saw him, he said: 'Madam, this time the gift I have for you needs some preparation.'

'What is it?'

'Let it be a surprise. But I will need your permission to bring a small camping stove. It's perfectly safe. The whole thing shouldn't take more than fifteen minutes.'

She was too intrigued to refuse and gave him a date and time when she knew that the launderette's owner was unlikely to turn up.

The Jamaican arrived at the arranged date and time, pulling a wheeled shopping bag. From the bag he took out a small stove and placed it on the counter, followed by a saucepan, oil, a box of eggs and what looked like two large bananas.

'These are not bananas,' he corrected her. 'They are plantains.'

He proceeded to peel the plantains, slice them diagonally, then fry them until they were golden-brown. Then he fried two eggs, and gave her, on a paper plate with a plastic fork, a portion of the dish he had prepared. The first mouthful slipped down her throat with a pleasant enough feeling, and the second mouthful made her smile inside and brought back warm memories of the early days when she was in love with her husband and could only see a future of happiness. She looked at the stranger with whom she was sharing this simple meal and said, 'Is nice, is very nice.'

'I know,' he said, and released a loud and deep laughter that sounded almost as delicious as the taste of the fried plantain and eggs on her tongue. Then suddenly, she felt a small tremor in her body and within seconds it had engulfed her, swallowed her whole and filled her with a forgotten pleasure and she had to excuse herself.

'Is anything wrong, madam?' the Jamaican said, anxiety on his face.

'No, no,' she said. 'I think I need some water. I have a bottle in the back.' Exercising the utmost self-control, her body alive with sensations, she went into the small office at the back of the launderette, closed the door and leaned against it, allowing the euphoric wave to freely surge through her until at last there was only the moisture of its passing and she was calm again and no longer felt an uncontrollable urge to groan and moan in rapturous pleasure. She took a swig of water and went back to join the stranger.

'Is very nice, this, this, plantain.'

'I am pleased you like it, madam,' he said, smiling at her with his eyes and lips, which both seemed to suggest that he knew what she had just experienced.

They finished the meal and, while repeating his instructions on the art of frying a plantain, he packed away his portable kitchen; then he left.

That autumn, not having seen the Jamaican since he had introduced her to the pleasure of the plantain – which was now a regular part of her meals, though it had never again so transported her as the first time she ate it – Olga was folding a customer's clothes when Martin came in. He, too, had been a stranger in recent weeks, and seeing him now she remembered his awkward advance, and realised how much courage it must have taken him. She watched him roughly push the clothes into the washing machine and shook her head in disapproval and despair. She put aside the shirt she was folding, walked over to Martin and said, 'I tell you many times, Martin. You have to balance the clothes in the machine. Let me do it for you.'

Martin moved aside, Olga adjusted the clothes, took the coins from Martin and said, 'Where have you been anyway?'

'Why do you want to know? What do you care where I've been?' Martin said.

'Maybe I have been missing you,' said the beautiful laundress.

Only for a While

1

When her dream of Caribbean retirement turned as sour as curdled milk, Sandra Barnes, née Miller, locked up her bungalow overlooking the Caribbean Sea and flew back to London, arriving at Heathrow Airport on a damp chilly Thursday morning in late February. Oscar, her son and only child, was there to meet her. They hugged, and she commented on his thinness, but her maternal solicitude appeared to fall on deaf ears as he dragged her suitcase towards the car park.

Few words passed between mother and son as they journeyed back into London. They had talked on the phone for several hours since she made her decision, and their penultimate conversation had ended in heated words. Oscar had called back, apologised and repeated his commitment to helping her. On hearing of the burglary and her decision to return to London, he had invited her to stay with him 'for a while' in his Stamford Hill house, where he lived alone. But, aggrieved by the caveat 'for a while', his mother had declined.

Sandra Barnes had given birth to Oscar when she was nineteen years old. She had married his English father, who absconded a year later, never to be seen again, brought up Oscar alone, inspired him to take his studies seriously by securing two degrees for herself, and if he had been the one in need of shelter, in spite of all her many sermons about the importance of being able to stand on his own two feet, she would have unhesitatingly and unconditionally taken him in.

Well, she would show him that her own spirit of independence and self-sufficiency was still alive. She was capable of finding somewhere to stay in London, though she hadn't visited in eighteen months. Sandra had been brought to London as a five-year-old and only left it when she was fifty-three, so she knew a vast network of people, many like her, single women who lived alone. Besides, she was only too well aware that her son's early success as a fabric designer - an unusual profession for which he had studied at the Slade School of Art, funded by his mother's generous financial and emotional support – had not been sustained. Oscar, who was nearing forty years of age, had the jaded, resigned air of someone who believed his best years were irreversibly behind him. She did not want to give him an opportunity to blame her for his stagnation.

On the next call, a week later, he had been conciliatory and had mentioned the vacant room in the Dalston apartment, his first property, bought with her help. Sandra had leapt at what seemed like an acceptable compromise.

It was in this apartment that Oscar deposited her. He showed her to her room, and then to the kitchen, where he opened the cupboard in which he had placed a few grocery items, coffee, tinned milk, malt biscuits. He knew she was a light and fussy eater. After he left – he had an appointment to keep, but promised to return the following morning – she took from her suitcase a plastic box containing sun-dried blue marlin and placed it in the fridge. She had brought a bottle of overproof white rum, and another of vintage dark rum; these she placed on the floor under the window, where they sat like apotropaic sentinels. Then she closed the curtains, changed into an oversized T-shirt and slipped into the single bed that Oscar had with prescient kindness made up for her.

Oscar had told her about the two other tenants, a woman who worked as a chef in a West End hotel, and a student – Indian or Sri Lankan, she couldn't remember. They knew she was due to move in that day. Early in the evening, shortly after the central heating came on, Sandra heard the woman enter the apartment. She had a vaguely Antipodean accent and her stentorian tones suggested that she might well have been speaking on her mobile phone to somebody in a billabong in the Australian outback.

Sandra was not yet ready to introduce herself. She was too tired, not to mention disoriented by what now seemed like too abrupt a transition from the tropics to the metropolis, from her vista over the Caribbean Sea to this tiny room behind Queensbridge Road. Her body straight and rigid beneath the duvet, she listened as the newcomer moved between kitchen and back bedroom. She dozed off and woke up in a silent house. She switched on the table lamp and began working on an unfinished electronic crossword puzzle. This was one of her favourite pastimes. She also owned an electronic dictionary to help her solve the more difficult clues, but used it only when she felt frustrated.

Soon afterwards the second tenant came home. She listened keenly as he opened the room door that was next to hers, came out and went to the bathroom on the other side of the corridor, then returned to his room. Silence reigned again.

Unable to sleep or read, she remained in bed roaming her memory. She remembered her home on the island, the implacable feeling of violation the burglary had caused, then days later, seeing a girl in the market wearing a cotton dress that resembled one she had once owned and had not seen for months, the growing suspicion that behind their friendly smiles and easy-going manners, the townspeople were envious of her privileges. This, even though she lived simply and frugally, her visits to London her sole indulgence. 'The English lady', some called her behind her back. It had been a lifelong dream, to return, but after four years the locals still treated her as a foreigner, as if some pungent and ineradicable odour emanated from her person. But she remained defiant: she planned to return around mid-September.

In the kitchen the following morning, Sandra met Kate, the Australian. She was dark-haired, fleshy, her cheeks florid with capillaries. Early thirties, Sandra estimated.

'Oscar told me you were coming. Knew you had arrived,' she said.

'How?'

'There's a fishy smell in the fridge.'

'Oh, that's my smoked marlin. Shouldn't smell, the box is air-tight.'

'It does, but then again, I've got a strong sense of smell.'

Sandra wasn't sure whether, in calling her attention to the smoked marlin, Kate was complaining.

'You'll get used to it,' she tried.

'Suppose so.'

Sandra thought Kate was brusque, but she made an effort to remain cordial. She wondered if Oscar and this plump Aussie were more than just landlord and tenant. It seemed unlikely, she thought, recalling her tall, alarmingly thin son who, as far as she knew, had not had a girlfriend since he was a teenager. What's more, in his early twenties he had declared that questions about his love-life were verboten. She gave the young woman what she hoped was a vaguely condescending smile.

'Right, off to work,' Kate said. She rinsed the cup from which she had drunk tea, placed it on the draining board, and left the kitchen.

When the front door slammed shut, Sandra opened the fridge and sniffed its interior. Detecting no offending smell she concluded that Kate could become a problem and consoled herself with the thought that staying in her son Oscar's flat was only a temporary arrangement.

As he had promised, Oscar came by around mid-morning, by which time Sandra had showered and changed her clothes. She made him a cup of tea and they sat at the round table in the kitchen, with Sandra's back to the window, facing Oscar. His thinness struck her again, but this time it did not alarm her. He had inherited her slender, elongated build and though his straight black hair gave him a vaguely Mediterranean appearance, there was no mistaking the family connection.

His mobile phone rang, and as he answered it she examined him further. She remembered spending much of her childhood wishing she were a boy, a desire that intensified when she entered her teens and grew five inches within fourteen months, becoming the tallest girl in secondary school. And when she gave birth to a son, she thought that her wish to be a boy had been fulfilled in a strange way.

'You don't look like somebody who's just come from the Caribbean,' Oscar said.

'Good. I didn't live here for most of my life without learning something about the British weather.'

'Actually, it's quite mild. We might have even turned the corner on winter. It hasn't snowed since early February, and I've even seen daffodils here and there.'

'The first daffodils are like a promise of fidelity from a serial adulterer,' Sandra said.

'Pleased to know that all that Caribbean sun hasn't blunted your wit, Mother. Anyway, I'm not stopping long. I have a lunch appointment; trying to get a contract to design a range for a new company. Sells only on the internet. A college friend of mine is on the inside.'

'Don't let me keep you, darling.'

'Is there anything you need?'

'I am fine. Thanks for asking. I need to go out myself. Put some credit on my phone, pick up some groceries.'

She accompanied him to the front door, where she said, 'Sunday lunch?' For many years, before her departure for the Caribbean, and on her previous visits to London, they had regularly met for Sunday lunch, occasions for her to gently probe him and tactfully offer advice that would help to make him the man she wanted him to be, as though he were an unfinished work of art, a sculpture maybe.

He hesitated, glanced away and replied: 'Could be tricky. I'll get back to you on that later.'

She felt a ripple of discomfort, which she soothed with the admission that she was at fault, being selfish and unrealistic. She had been away for eighteen months, the longest gap between her London visits, now this sudden return, and she expected them to slip into their past routine. She murmured a soft 'Okay', kissed his cheeks and said goodbye.

With Oscar gone she went into the living room and was struck by the sparse furniture and general air of disuse. The curtains were closed, a single mattress covered in clear plastic stood in an alcove and there wasn't even a television. She sat in a beige corduroy-covered armchair, reflecting on the discomfiture he had unwittingly caused her, or she had caused herself. And in that moment of reflection, a disturbing thought strayed into her mind: that the burglary had been a mere pretext for leaving the island and returning to London. She dismissed the thought.

The sound of a door opening and closing reminded her that she was not alone in the flat.

The other tenant, Rajiv, the student, was still at home. Sandra remained still and listened as he went into the bathroom. On hearing the bathroom door being bolted, she went into her room and lay on the bed. She remained there as Rajiv, or the person she believed was Rajiv, moved between the bathroom, bedroom and kitchen. She wanted to go out and introduce herself, but a curious mixture of shyness and enervation kept her pinned to the bed, one leg on the floor. When she heard the front door close, she got up and readied herself to go out.

Sandra walked to Dalston Junction under a low grey and white sky. She noted the new station, the piazza and apartments, which she thought resembled shipping containers, vertically and horizontally stacked and clad in wood. She tried to remember what was there before the redevelopment but her memory yielded a blank, an increasingly familiar but no less disconcerting occurrence, and for an instant her mind was filled with a portentous image of herself, a senescent amnesiac, wandering through a maze of streets in some unknown city of cloud-high shipping containers.

She turned on to Kingsland Road, and above the roar of the traffic heard French, Spanish and Portuguese, Italian, Yoruba and other, unrecognisable, languages being spoken by pedestrians as they streamed past, swerving to avoid each other.

In the shopping mall, she bought some credit for her mobile phone but realised that she had not charged the phone. Connecting with her London friends would have to wait. She left the mobile phone shop and headed towards the supermarket, then decided that if she shopped there now, she would have to go home immediately afterwards, and she wasn't quite ready to be back inside. So she left the mall and drifted across the top of Ridley Road market. And it felt good to be back in London, to be just another face in a crowd, lost in the anonymity that only a large city can give.

She walked as far as the Rio Cinema, crossed the road and saw that a French film was showing; maybe later in the week she would come and watch the movie. She had last seen a film at the Spanish Club in Portland. She walked back towards Dalston, and then turned into Gillett Street and was disappointed to see that the little Ethiopian coffee kiosk was closed. The bar below the Vortex Jazz Bar on Gillett Square was open, though, and she went inside, ordered a caffè latte and took a seat on a high chair that gave her a view of the length of the square. She had been sitting there for a while, thinking about nothing more than how much she was looking forward to reconnecting with one or two female friends, when she heard a male voice say: 'Sandra Barnes?'

She glanced to her left and saw a man she didn't recognise but felt she ought to know because he knew her name. She gave a hesitant, suspicious reply.

'Yes?'

'Niall Harding. Goldsmiths, way back when.'

'Oh, of course,' she said. 'Forgive me, I was miles away.' His mention of a place somehow made him seem less of a stranger, and it stirred a vague and tantalisingly elusive memory. She had been a part-time student at the South London college, undertaken a trek two days each week for five years, leaving Oscar with her mother.

'Nothing to forgive,' he said. 'Such a long time ago. Did you ever finish the course?'

'Yes, then did another, a bit closer to home, though. And you?'

'Oh yeah, I finished. Did a few more part-time courses, evening courses, that sort of thing. Couldn't afford any more full-time studies. Had to work.'

'What did you do?'

'Ended up working for the fire service, admin side. Took early retirement last year.'

'Sounds as if you're a success.'

He laughed lightly. 'Tell that to my wife, rather ex-wife. We're separated but not divorced. Said she had devoted her life to a loser, an also-ran. She's a very ambitious woman.'

'Ambitious for what?'

'Not sure, actually. Don't think she knew, either. Anyway, what about you – married? Children? Still working?'

'No, to the first and last. One child. And you, do you have children?'

'Yes, two. One's now living in the States, and the other one, well ... the less said about her the better. Is this your neighbourhood, Dalston?'

'No, no, I'm just visiting my son. Visiting from Jamaica.'

'Oh, you live in Jamaica. Lucky you.'

Niall was London-born of Trinidadian and Antiguan parents, and a few years younger than Sandra. He was tall and straight, smoothly shaved, his face oiled. He had the volubility of one who spent many days by himself. Niall now told her that he sometimes travelled on the 149 bus from his home in Tottenham Green to Ridley Road market; at other times he went as far as London Bridge for a walk beside the river or to roam around the City of London.

'You never thought of going home?' Sandra asked.

'Home? I *am* home,' Niall said emphatically.

His reply seemed to possess solidity, like a block of stone or a slab of metal, and it made her acknowledge that she could not call anywhere home with the same unshakeable conviction or comparable megalithic certainty. Yes, she called 'the island' home, but she lacked the sort of absolute sense of it being home that was audible in Niall's voice. So often she still felt as though she were on a chimerical quest, a nugatory pursuit inspired by grief at her mother's death. And now time was running out on her. How much time? She'd be sixty soon. How much time did she have?

They walked together back to Kingsland High Road and she waited with him at the bus stop in front of an Asian-owned grocery store, its plantains, aubergines and yams spilling out onto the pavement. They exchanged telephone numbers. His bus came. She stood and watched him board it, noting his blue jeans, black leather jacket and brown boots, the practical clothes of an urban walker. He looks after himself, she thought. I like that.

Afterwards, she shopped for some groceries in Sainsbury's and then took a minicab home.

2

Sandra woke up in a silent house and thought it was evening before she checked her watch and saw that it was 23:35. Thankfully, her room was warm. She sat up in bed, wondering how she had managed to sleep for so many hours through the comings and goings in the house, and settled on jet-lag as a plausible explanation. The bedside lamp, a white Anglepoise, reflected off the wardrobe mirror and filled the room with a crepuscular light. She disconnected her now fully charged phone from the mains and checked for messages: Oscar had sent her a text. She didn't feel like reading it just yet.

She took a sip of water from a bottle. And with the water coursing down her throat, she remembered the encounter with Niall - and the memory of their easy conversation came to her with warmth and, for some inexplicable reason, the scent of cinnamon. She allowed herself a smile, and wondered if she would ever hear from him. It seemed unlikely. Many years had passed since she had been intimate with a man. It wasn't for want of opportunities, but she seemed to be desired by the wrong sort of men, married, promiscuous, excited by her veneer of exoticism; and she herself desired the wrong sort of men, married and sober, too settled into domesticity for amorous adventures. In any case, love had never been her most trustworthy visitor, always bringing chaos and tumult and upheaval, like a hurricane.

She got out of bed, turned on the ceiling light and stood before the narrow wardrobe mirror. She took off her T-shirt and began examining herself. The white roots of her low-cropped hair were beginning to show - time to visit the hairdresser - and her face was as dry as onion skin. Her fingers were her least attractive feature, too stubby, and her long fingernails, thickened and reddened by layers of nail polish, far from rendering them beautiful, made them look like the talons of a raptor. She had long forsworn bras, didn't own any, preferring loose blouses or, on special occasions, halter necks. And time had eroded her hips and buttocks.

She remembered a colour photograph taken on Brighton beach, of her bikini-clad sixteen-year-old self: proud breasts, narrow waist, flared hips, long legs – the pier in the distant background. Since then, since that moment of physical perfection, she had been in slow decline, an irreversible metamorphosis, partly willed, into this middle-aged woman, epicene and dishevelled most of the time but, despite the severity of her own self-criticism, utterly at ease with her body.

She put the T-shirt back on and went to the bathroom. She brushed her teeth and washed her face, and then went back to bed, where she roamed her memory again until the nocturnal thrum of the city became a bass-driven lullaby, reassuring and soporific.

3

On Sunday morning Sandra received a fleeting visit from Oscar, bearing a bunch of limp, etiolated roses. He had told her on the phone that he had a business appointment in Birmingham.

'On a Sunday?' she had said.

'Makes no difference nowadays.'

Now she noted his apologetic air as he presented her with the flowers.

'When will you be back?' she asked.

'Early evening. We could meet then. I'll probably be knackered though.'

'You know I don't like rushed Sundays.'

'Thought I'd offer anyway. We'll have lunch next Sunday. Definitely.'

'Drive safely.'

She stood on the front porch and watched him drive off in his blue soft-top Saab, and when the car disappeared from sight she felt an anguish that was exacerbated by the ageing flowers and the grey morning light. She returned to her room and lay on the bed, wondering how she could have produced such an obtuse young man. He had known that she would be in London. He ought to have kept her first Sunday back clear, so they could catch up, so she could fuss over him, recount her adventures on the island. Was that too much to ask?

She felt tears welling up and fought them back. She reached for her phone, as if for a palliative pill, and began scrolling through her list of contacts. She stopped at Niall's number and as her thumb hovered over 'call', suddenly she became aware of her own absurdity. She was behaving like a petulant teenager. She tossed the phone aside on the bed and silently urged herself to calm down. She reminded herself that her sixtieth birthday was only seventeen months away, an impending landmark that she had in recent times appealed to as another layer of integument against the casual and often unwitting hurt that people visited on each other every day. And with that reminder, she recalled the severe sermons she had delivered to Oscar, always repeating: 'Look after yourself, look after number one.'

Unexpectedly, the phone rang. She snatched it up, saw that it was Niall, executed a swift act of self-composure and then answered.

'Hello, Sandra? I was wondering whether you'd like to go for a walk or see a movie this afternoon.'

'Oh, Niall, that's a great offer. Got to take a rain check though. I am spending the afternoon with my son. Lunch. Catching up. That sort of thing.'

'Maybe sometime next week?'

'Yes, good idea. Towards the end of the week might be possible. I'll call you or you can call me.'

'Will do.'

She put the phone aside, got off the bed, stood before the mirror and, hands raised, flicked her thumbs on her forefingers and whispered a triumphantly sibilant, 'Yesss.'

4

'The strangest thing happened to me last week,' Sandra said, pausing for effect. She was having Sunday lunch with Oscar, in his rambling late-Victorian house in Stamford Hill. She gazed up at the small original Winston Branch painting she had given her son for his thirtieth birthday. It was one of several original works of art, all gifts from her, in a room whose walls were otherwise dominated by mirrors of various shapes and sizes. Oscar was sitting below the painting on a black leather sofa; she was in a matching armchair.

'Strange things are always happening to you, Mother,' Oscar said.

'No, this was *really* strange.'

'What was it?'

'Actually, it wasn't last week. It was the week before.'

'Yes?'

'I met a man. Somebody I should have known in the past but didn't. We met in Dalston, the day after I arrived. We had dinner on Thursday evening.'

'Where?'

'Little Thai restaurant on Church Street.'

'What's strange about a man taking you out to dinner?'

'Well, what's strange is that I quite like him.' She scrutinised her son's face for a reaction. The slightest hint of jealousy would have satisfied her.

'He passed your cutlery test, then?'

'He used chopsticks, actually.' Sandra laughed at their private joke. Years ago, disappointed by a prospective lover, she had told Oscar that she had terminated the relationship because the man never placed his knife and fork together at the end of a meal. She could not now remember how Niall had placed his chopsticks, only his impressive dexterity with implements that always frustrated her. But her laughter concealed serious intent. She was trying to nudge the conversation towards Oscar's own love-life, to know whether her cherished hope of a grandchild was any closer to being fulfilled.

As if he knew exactly what she was leading up to, Oscar said, 'I saw Jacqueline, in the week.'

'How is she?'

'Fine. And Nick. We went to the movies together.'

'Two's company, three's a ...'

'Nick invited me.'

Sandra fell silent. Jacqueline was Oscar's childhood friend and their closeness had survived her six-year marriage to Nick, a City worker. Oscar had even accompanied them on holidays, to the south of Spain, the Riviera and Rome. Sandra found his single status and continuing relationship with Jacqueline as part of a ménage à trois disturbing.

'No child on the way for Jackie? Time's running out for her.'

'Don't think they're planning to have any.'

'What is the matter with your generation? No wonder Britain has to bring in so many foreign workers.'

'Are you saying that my generation is in dereliction of our national duty by failing to breed?'

'Breed? Animals breed, Oscar. Human beings ...'

'... breed also.'

Sandra regretted having steered their conversation in this direction. She just wanted a pleasant Sunday afternoon with her son. The burglary had been an ordeal, the persistent feeling of violation, palpable long after she had changed and upgraded the locks, the suspicion that the same people who greeted her in the town with their broad smiles knew exactly who the culprits were, her arduous efforts to maintain an appearance of composure. She had not flown all this way to argue with her only child. But there was something about the word 'breed', something accusatory and reproachful, resounding with echoes of past exchanges, rancorous, circular and inconclusive, about his absent father.

'What are you trying to say, Oscar? Speak your mind – I can take it. Do you think that's how you came into the world, an offspring of two animals breeding?'

Oscar got up and walked to the mantelpiece, his reflection in the large curved mirror.

'I am waiting for an answer, Oscar.'

'You don't seriously expect me to answer that question?'

'Yes, I do.'

'You're the only one who can answer that question, Mother.'

Sandra felt a choking sensation, as if something or somebody had seized her throat. She got up from the armchair, walked over to Oscar, looked into his dark brown eyes, and said, 'I know I haven't always been a good mother, but you mean everything to me. Everything.'

'We weren't talking about your qualities as a mother. But I suppose everything always comes back to you.'

'Meaning?'

'I don't know what I mean. Let's just leave it there.'

'It seems to me that there's something you want to say to me, something of great importance to you. I am not going to press you. Take your time. And whenever you're ready to say whatever it is you want to say but feel you can't say right now, I will listen, as I have always done.'

'Okay. Let's leave it there, all right? Anyway, I have more urgent things to think about. I didn't get the contract I was chasing.'

'Oh, darling, I am sorry. Why didn't you say?'

'Because ... it will have repercussions – not getting the contract. I need to maximise the rent from the flat. May even have to let out rooms here.'

'No. Don't let out rooms in your home. You didn't spend three years in art college in order to become a landlord.'

'I don't think I'll have much of choice, Mother.'

'Something will turn up. Meanwhile, I'll pay you for the room in Dalston. Whatever the going rate is.'

'I can't take rent from you.'

'No. I insist. I insist.'

That night, as she lay awake waiting for sleep to claim her, Sandra remembered her teenage pregnancy, the bewildered young man who persuaded her to marry him in a registry office then fled, keeping in touch for the first five years of Oscar's life by depositing money in her bank account, money that she always put aside for her son's future. Then even that contact stopped. It all seemed so distant, as if it had happened in some other lifetime, or even to somebody else. But Oscar, for whom she felt a love beyond mere words, and his ability to wound her, was proof of that past.

5

A month passed. Sandra was walking with Niall in Finsbury Park, below an opalescent afternoon sky. The temperature was mild, the park grass a shimmering mixture of green and yellow in the sunlight, in the shade a dark, brooding green. Having bloomed for a few weeks, the daffodils were now clusters of headless floppy stalks. The couple stopped beside the athletics grounds and watched two runners circling the ochre-coloured track, then leaned on the fence. They were talking about a film they had seen some weeks before when her phone rang.

'Excuse me.' She stepped away from Niall. 'Leaving? Why? ... I've never seen him ... Two weeks' notice. Okay. Talk to you soon, darling.' She rejoined Niall.

'Anything wrong?'

'No. No. Just one of the tenants in the Dalston flat. He's vacating the room. That was Oscar.'

'A strange arrangement. You say Oscar lives alone in a whole house. Why aren't you staying with him?'

'Oh, I couldn't do that, at least not for more than a few weeks. This way I don't have to worry about moving again before returning to Jamaica. Last time I was here I stayed in four different places, including a spell with Oscar, over six months.'

'I still don't get it,' Niall said. 'When I visited my daughter in Connecticut last year I stayed for a whole month.'

'I am here for six months. It'd be a burden on Oscar.'

'At least now I understand why you were such a scarce figure on the campus.'

'Were you looking for me?'

'Not exactly. But you were a striking figure. You aroused curiosity.'

'And now, I am no longer a striking figure.'

'I am not saying that. Now I am even more curious. What happened to your son's father?'

'That's a tough question. I can't give you an answer right now, but I will one day.'

'Fair enough,' he said evenly. 'You brought up your son, brought him up well, for him to become a success. So I don't imagine you topped his father and buried him under the patio.'

'Actually, it was at the end of the garden.'

She laughed lightly. She was reminded of what she liked about him, his easy-going manners. She had seen some of her old friends – Yvonne in Brockley, Cecille in Streatham, Camilla in Edmonton – but only once. None could compete with Niall for her attention; they had met up as often as three times a week. She switched off her phone; she'd been enjoying her stroll with Niall and didn't want any further disturbances. Since their last date, she had decided that she liked him enough to make him a lover, perhaps her last; someone to hold her body, infuse it with a half-forgotten pleasure, and leave her with an indelibly warm memory that could soothe the aches and pains of impending old age. But how to make the transition from friendship to physical intimacy was proving difficult.

A week before, on a full-moon night, she had spent hours in his home listening to music; they had even danced together to a Luther Vandross track. In the past, in some dank and dark oubliette of her memory, she was sure that close dancing in private was frequently a prelude to love-making, a signpost for the evening's ineluctable destination. It had not happened. At the end of the dance he had thanked her with theatrical formality, then, using a remote control device on a multi-CD player, he had changed the music and the mood. Soon afterwards, with the time approaching 2 a.m., he had called a cab for her. She had asked the driver to drop her at Dalston station and chosen to walk home from there, now and again gazing up at the sidereal sky, disappointed and yet elated by the stirring of long-dormant feelings. Next time, she thought, I will have to take the lead, be proactive. Administer some philtre if necessary. If that doesn't work, find a nepenthe and accept the immutable order of things. Meanwhile, she would drop hints of her desire.

They walked away from the athletics track, towards the café. She moved close to him, linked arms with him, shivered and said, 'It's getting cold.' And when he stepped into her stride and pressed his body close, she felt the immeasurable joy of anticipation.

6

In early May, after three consecutive days of rain, the temperature rose and greenery seemed to explode everywhere in London. Niall was visiting his brother in Leeds and Sandra now found herself with many empty days, which she filled with gardening. The back garden of the flat had obviously once enjoyed attention. There were two rose bushes near the house, and a fenced area that might once have served as a kitchen garden but was now a large bed of desiccated plants with spring growth here and there. To one side of the garden was a builder's yard; rusting scaffolding and planks of timber pierced the air above a wall covered in a riotously sprawling ivy, which also covered the entire back wall. Using a set of tools she had found in a kitchen cupboard, Sandra stripped the walls of the ivy, weeded the concrete path and turned the soil in the bed where she planned to plant herbs, tomatoes, lettuces, carrots and courgettes.

As she worked she thought about Niall and their nights together. The first had been disastrous, all awkward fumbling and a stubborn dryness that made her fear an infarction due to age or disuse. But Niall, tender, patient and playful, had given a whole new meaning to the phrase 'speaking in tongues' with his fearless fluency, and on the second occasion her body flooded with such exquisite sensations that she felt like an arid riverbed at the end of a long, too long, dry season. In this exultant mood, among the spring shoots, Sandra began to wonder whether she should return to London permanently.

This afternoon, she was taking a break from her horticultural labours to interview a prospective tenant for the room vacated by the mysterious Rajiv, whom she had never met. Oscar could not be present; he had given her instructions to show the caller, another Asian student, the room and pass on any observations she had to make about his suitability.

Recognising another opportunity to make herself useful to Oscar, to lighten the burden of the numerous responsibilities of being a landlord, and thereby create more space and time for him to pursue his difficult profession, Sandra had accepted this duty with alacrity.

Mr Yusuf Kamesh arrived punctually at 2 p.m. He was in his late twenties, had thick jet-black hair, the pock-marked face of someone who had suffered chickenpox in his infancy, and carried a rucksack that, like his blue jeans and grey plastic windcheater, still carried the scent of the shop from which they must have been recently purchased.

She showed him the room, which she had cleaned, and he nodded in approval, then she showed him the kitchen and bathroom. She could not identify exactly what it was that made her feel uneasy about Yusuf Kamesh. His whispering voice, his stealthy footfall as he followed her about the flat, his politeness – whatever it was, she felt compelled to find out more about him. Oscar had told her he was a postgraduate student at one of the University of London colleges and had seen the ad for the room on the college's accommodation noticeboard.

In the living room, she said, 'The apartment belongs to my son. I am staying here temporarily and the other tenant at the moment is an Australian woman. But I suppose Oscar has told you all that?'

'Yes, yes. That's all fine with me.'

'It's a bit late in the academic year to be searching for a room,' she said.

'I've been away, doing fieldwork. I am a geologist.'

'Where were you?'

He hesitated, then replied, 'Pakistan.'

'I see.' Sandra heard the faint peals of an alarm bell, as if her absent son was in danger. She walked Yusuf Kamesh to the front door where, without premeditation, she said in what she hoped was a lighthearted tone, 'I hope you're not a jihadist.'

Yusuf Kamesh visibly bristled. He straightened himself up, glared at her and said with punctilious politeness, 'Thank you, Mrs Oscar. I will let Mr Oscar know if I want the room. It's a very nice room.'

Sandra chided herself as she closed the front door. Thoughtless, paranoid fool.

She returned to the garden, resumed bagging the plants she had weeded, and waited for the irate telephone call she knew was bound to come.

'You have just caused me to lose a tenant. You know I need to rent the room asap.'

'I'm sorry, Oscar. There was something about him – I can't say what. Anyway, you can't be certain he was going to take it.'

'Look, Mother, you're beginning to get in the way. You know why Rajiv left, don't you?'

'I had nothing to do with Rajiv's departure.'

'Yes, you did, Mother. He said he saw you walking naked along the corridor late at night, and for that reason couldn't stay there any more.'

'That's not true, Oscar.'

'Well, that's what he told me. You scared him off. Satisfied? Scared him off. I'm going. I have things to do.'

'Oscar, that is simply not true ...' It took her a few seconds to realise that her son had hung up.

Sandra walked back to the kitchen. She was used to Oscar's abrupt ending of their conversations but this last one had a new level of force. She drank a glass of water to help calm her frayed nerves, and consoled herself with the thought that he would probably call back in the evening. She would explain then, as she always did when they fought, that she had his best interests at heart. But for now their contretemps had left her distressed and in need of rest. She decided to eat a light lunch before taking a siesta. A slice of smoked marlin on toast would do.

She opened the fridge and reached for the plastic box but saw only an empty space. A closer inspection confirmed that the plastic box was gone. She slammed the fridge door and tried to remember when she last ate a slice of the delicacy she had brought from Jamaica. Three days ago. Then, in a moment of startling clarity, she realised what had happened to the smoked marlin. 'That bitch,' she spat out.

She made do with a boiled egg on toast, then retired to her room where, lying on the bed, she worked herself up into a fury that was only partially cooled by an hour's sleep.

'It stank. I couldn't take it any more, so I threw it away.'

She had waited for Kate to come in from work, and now cornered her in the kitchen.

'You had no business throwing away something that was not your property. You should have told me.'

'I told you when you first arrived. It smelled then, and over four months on, the stench was unbearable. I didn't think it was edible.'

'That was for me to decide. Not you.'

'I am a chef. I know when food is off, when it should be junked.'

'It was not your ... I am going to complain to ...' With her son's name on the tip of her tongue, Sandra suddenly became aware of the futility of the argument. Her prized smoked blue marlin was gone. It was a fait accompli, and no amount of heated words would bring it back. This young woman, this child, younger than her son, had humiliated her. And after her faux pas earlier in the day,

Oscar was bound to interpret a row between her and Kate as yet another instance of interference in his business.

'I probably saved you from food poisoning,' Kate said, brushing past her.

The sound of Kate's bedroom door slamming shut and the key being turned shook Sandra out of the shock caused by the young woman's effrontery.

7

Niall returned from the north of England and Sandra saw him once, and pleasurably, before another family emergency – this time his elderly mother – began to consume his time. Text messages and short telephone conversations replaced their trysts. She busied herself with the garden and worked on repairing the various relations she had ruptured. To Kate she presented an amiable and forgiving face. Kate in turn apologised for her high-handed ejection of the stale marlin and presented Sandra with a package of Scottish oak-smoked salmon. Oscar was less easily appeased. That she, Sandra, might have caused him to lose a tenant was the source of a smidgen of guilt, which she assuaged by reminding herself that she had acted in his best interest. Despite several viewings, the room remained empty, while she stayed on and tried to keep Oscar optimistic that it would be occupied by late summer.

Sometimes she met up with friends, gossiped over dinner or lunch, graciously received their compliments on her healthy glow, reassured them that they had no reason to envy her transatlantic lifestyle. And if she received a text message from Niall while dining, she would give a salacious titter, like a naughty schoolgirl, which would open a new channel of conversation. It was after one of these lunches – this time in a Wood Green Italian restaurant – that she found herself facing the prospect of an empty afternoon stretching into an even more vacant evening. The garden did not need any more work, she had not heard from Niall for a few days, and she did not feel like going straight back to Dalston. So when her friend Camilla Ford, who owned a car and lived in Edmonton, offered to drop her somewhere, she accepted the offer and gave the Tottenham Bus Garage as a drop-off point.

She began walking towards Seven Sisters with Tottenham Green on her right, and beyond the red-brick municipal buildings. But when she glanced across the busy road, to the crescent of tall houses where Niall lived, she noticed that his living-room window was open. The day was warm, but not so warm that you would go out and leave the window open, even one on the second floor. She crossed the road. As she neared the front door, a man came out and she rushed past him to catch the door before it closed.

She knocked at Niall's door and waited and thought she smelled incense, some sort of musk. Then she thought she heard a female voice say something like, 'I hope it's the takeaway we ordered.'

A key turned, and the door flew open and Sandra stood face to face with a woman in her late twenties with tousled hair, smeared lipstick, and wearing – only wearing, it seemed – a striped cotton shirt with the upper buttons undone, exposing a fleshy, golden-brown cleavage that matched the other exposed parts of her body.

Sandra's left elbow tightened on her handbag and she said with an icy calm, 'Is Niall home?'

The young woman shot her an insolent look, then shouted over her shoulder, 'Niall, it's not the takeaway. There's a lady here for you.' Leaving the door open, she turned and walked away. She was barefooted and her muscular calves flowed into firm, evenly-toned thighs that disappeared under the shirt.

Presently Niall stood before her. His torso was bare, and a lungi covered his lower half.

'Sandra!' he exclaimed. 'What are you doing here? I told you I'd be busy today.'

'Yes, visiting your elderly mother. You lying ...' She could not finish the sentence and in the pause she reached for a familiar weapon and said, 'You tergiversate, sir.'

He gave her a blank look of incomprehension.

'Maybe you'll understand this,' she said, and her arm shot forward, as if in a massive involuntary twitch, and slapped Niall on his left cheek, throwing his face towards the floor.

He shook his head and ran a hand down his cheek then looked at his palm, which was smeared with blood, the result of a nick from one of Sandra's long, lacquered fingernails.

Sandra saw the blood on his hand, the incision on his cheek, gasped and recoiled.

'You'd better go home, Sandra,' Niall said. 'I was being kind to you. Just being kind. Nothing else. Go home.'

She turned and fled down the stairs and out of the house into the warm June afternoon, along Tottenham High Road towards Seven Sisters tube station, the deafening sound of traffic flowing into and out of the city a mechanical and cruelly indifferent musical accompaniment to an inner turmoil that owed as much to the wound inflicted by her perfidious lover as his commanding her to go home – because in her hurt she felt utterly homeless, trapped in a never-ending state of transition, some kind of purgatory beyond which lay neither heaven nor hell.

8

Sandra had not reached what she liked to regard – prematurely, she was aware – as her 'great age' without developing a quality of resilience. Betrayed in love, she retreated to her son's Dalston flat and concentrated on gardening and improving the appearance of the unused living room. From charity and second-hand furniture shops between Dalston and Church Street she bought several items to give the place a more lived-in feel: two mirrors with rococo wrought-iron frames and, as a concession to her son, an original painting in the style of Mondrian executed by a local artist. She saw little of Kate, but on the rare occasions when they met in the kitchen, she enjoyed the chef's companionship, and decided that Kate was an acquired taste. At the end of each day, usually around 7 p.m., Sandra retired to her bedroom and listened to the documentaries and dramas on Radio 4, or music on Radio 3, on a portable stereo/radio; or worked on a crossword puzzle. This way an entire month passed, during which time her wounded heart healed.

When she felt satisfied with her handiwork on the living room, she decided to start returning the hospitality her London friends had shown her. She invited Ella Robson to lunch. She had known Ella for over thirty years, their friendship having started as a febrile one-night exploration in sapphic love. After lunch they settled down in the living room, and Sandra told her friend about the disastrous incident in Tottenham with Niall. Ella laughed and said, 'You should have asked them for a threesome, my dear,' and while they were still laughing, Sandra received a telephone call from her friend Camilla who, shopping in Dalston with a friend, Kadija, wondered whether she wanted to join them. Sandra explained that she had a visitor and reversed the invitation.

Half an hour later, Sandra found herself hosting an extempore party. She brought from the bedroom the portable stereo and what remained of the bottle of over-proof white rum, from which she had taken a few medicinal sips since arriving in London. Camilla brought in CDs from her car and a bottle of Spanish red wine. Immured in the company of these old friends, with music playing and alcohol flowing, washed by their fruity laughter, Sandra felt, for the first time in many years, if not at home, then certainly nearing home. And the inchoate idea of returning to London which had come to her while gardening in the spring now took more solid form. Her house in the Caribbean seemed far-off and desolate. Next time she had lunch with Oscar, she would broach the subject, drop hints. She could run this flat, lighten his load.

When Kate came in from work, she stuck her head round the door, and Sandra introduced her to her friends. She invited Kate to join them, but Kate tactfully pleaded tiredness.

In acknowledgement of Kate's presence in the house, Sandra turned down the music, though she could do nothing about Camilla's loud voice, which rivalled Kate's bellowing on the telephone. But she soon forgot that she and her visitors were no longer alone. When the bottle of red wine was finished, Camilla revealed that she had another three in the car and was prepared to fetch them. There was some hesitation before the others gave their consent. With the new bottles of wine, the volume of the music crept up, and the conversation became louder, and time passed more swiftly.

Sandra went to the kitchen to fetch a pitcher of water for her friends and found Kate standing there dressed in a knee-length nightshirt.

'I hope your party's going to finish soon,' Kate said.

'Oh, are we disturbing you, darling?' Sandra said. She was tipsy, merry. 'I'm sorry. We should be finished soon. I'll make sure to turn down the music.'

'Good. You know I wake early for work.'

'I said I'm sorry, Kate.'

'That's not good enough. You're disturbing me.'

'Okay, I hear you, Kate.'

Kate returned to her room and Sandra rejoined her friends. In her absence, the conversation had moved on and the guests were now discussing the latest dance craze. Camilla's friend, Kadija, had attended that year's Trinidad carnival, and having seen what she considered an absurd new dance trend that was typical of the younger generation, wanted to demonstrate it; she asked if she could turn up the volume on the stereo. Sandra agreed to it being increased a little, for only a minute. When this was done, Camilla gave a brief demonstration of robotic movements, which caused the room to erupt in riotous laughter. Sandra turned down the music again.

Whether it was the long summer evening, or the unusual experience of being in the company of so many women her own age, Sandra could not say. But she had no desire to see them go, disperse to their flats and houses around the city. She could not remember when she had been in such convivial company.

Suddenly she saw Kate standing in the living-room doorway. She was holding a stick with a rounded head. Before Sandra could react, Kate entered the room, walked up to the portable stereo, which was on the floor, and smashed it with the stick. Sandra later learned the stick was what South Africans called a knobkerrie.

'I asked you politely to turn down the music,' Kate said. Then she turned, marched out of the room.

The four women had frozen on her entrance, and Camilla was the first to speak.

'What? What was *that*?' she said.

Sandra, now recovering, said, 'I think we'd better call it a night, ladies.'

When her friends left, Sandra retired to her bed and fell asleep instantly. The following morning, she woke up with a rare hangover, surveyed the living room, with the empty wine bottles and smashed stereo, and went back to bed until early afternoon. She emerged from sleep with one thought: If I am going to make this place my home, that young woman has to go.

9

That evening she received a telephone call from Oscar.

'She complained that you held a party there.'

'It was just a few friends. They dropped in. It wasn't planned. And we were not noisy.'

'She said that you and your friends were making a lot of noise and that you ignored her appeals to stop.'

'I did not ignore her. And what she did to the stereo, *your* stereo, was unwarranted. Excessive. Downright brutal.'

'Mother, don't you think I have enough on my plate as it is without having to mediate between you and Kate? I don't need it, Mother. I do not need it.'

'But you seem prepared to believe her version of events over mine.'

'You know very well that in the two years she has been there she's been an extremely reliable tenant. She pays her rent on time and doesn't cause me, or the other tenants, any trouble.'

'And I am your mother, and I am telling you what happened yesterday evening.'

Sandra heard a groan of exasperation, then silence as the phone went down at the other end. Ordinarily, she would have waited for Oscar to call back and apologise. But on this occasion, imbued with a sense of being wronged, she could not wait. She rang him back immediately. She got his answering service, and left a message in which she poured out years of frustration and hurt that she had not known she was carrying. Exhausted by her rant, she lay on the bed, fighting back tears. A few minutes later, the phone rang, with Oscar's name displayed. She answered it.

'I think it's time for you to either go back to Jamaica, or stay with one of your friends here in London.'

'Are you kicking me out, Oscar?'

'I am asking you to leave the flat, Mother. You were only meant to stay for a while and you have been there for ages. That's why I have not been able to rent the room. You caused Rajiv to leave, walking around naked. And with you in the place, nobody wants the room. Next thing, Kate will leave.'

'Are you choosing that - that *sheila* over me?'

'Her name is Kate. And I quite like her. She's an excellent tenant, and I don't want to lose her.'

'You *are* choosing her over me. I carried you for nine months in my body, I made you the person you are.'

'I am not just the result of your breeding, Mother; I played some part in making myself.'

At the sound of the word 'breeding', the taut, tenuous strings that were holding Sandra together snapped. 'You, you vain, ungrateful ...'

After two minutes of unrelenting ranting, Sandra realised that she was talking to herself. Trembling, she threw the phone aside and rushed into the garden and the fresh air. When she felt more composed, she returned to her room and stayed there, sitting upright on the bed, sometimes poring over a crossword puzzle. Kate's arrival from work barely impinged on her consciousness.

From that day, time passed in a blur for Sandra. She had a vague memory of two visitors, male and female, both claiming to be doctors, visiting the apartment on separate occasions and quizzing her. And one early evening, at the end of the long-drawn-out dusk, with Sandra trying and failing to make progress on a crossword puzzle, the flat doorbell rang. She was not expecting a visitor, so ignored it in the hope that somebody else would answer the door. The bell rang again. She remained sitting upright on the bed. But when it rang again, a third time, followed by banging on the door, she got off the bed, put on her slippers and wrapped herself in a red cashmere shawl.

Approaching the front door, she saw two figures through the frosted glass. She opened it to find a woman there. A man stood a step behind her; they both wore uniforms. There was an ambulance parked in front of the house and a police car in front of the ambulance.

'Good evening. Mrs Barnes?' the man asked and she nodded.

'Oscar Barnes, your son, sent us,' the woman explained.

'My son sent you? Oscar Barnes, my son, sent you?'

'Yes, he sent us. You have to come with us.'

'I'll come with you, if Oscar sent you. Did Oscar send you?' she repeated quietly.

'Yes, your son, Oscar Barnes, sent us. He wants you to come with us.'

The woman reached forward and touched her shoulder, and Sandra gathered the shawl around her body and folded her arms. She stepped over the threshold and closed the front door, and the woman took one of her elbows. The man took her other elbow. They held her gently and she felt safe – and experienced a curious light-headedness, a feeling of being somehow absent from the moment, as if she were floating above it all and observing some facsimile of her own body.

She was led to the gate. A crowd had gathered, neighbours and passers-by. The night obscured their faces. Looming above them, at the back of the crowd, was a tall, thin figure, his face hidden beneath a blue hoodie.

She stopped walking and said, 'Oscar sent you?'

'Yes, Mrs Barnes, your son sent us.'

As she stepped up into the ambulance, she glanced back at the crowd, searching for the tall hooded figure, and thought she saw an outline of a person in the space where he had been standing but he, whoever he was, was not there any more.

Friends and Ex-Lovers

He is standing in Regent's Park, waiting for a friend. He spots her approaching along a north-south footpath, a petite, middle-aged woman walking with a brisk jauntiness. She is wearing a green, sleeveless, striped cotton pinafore dress. Her arms, calves and face have a uniform paleness, which seems more pronounced because many people surrounding her are tanned and, this being twenty-first-century London, most are naturally brown or dark. She has put on weight in recent years, acquired a pleasant roundness. He remembers when they were lovers, her girlish figure, always pale, her round cheeks.

Seeing him, she smiles, waves and hurries towards him. They hug and brush cheeks. She smells of soap and shampoo.

'Sorry I'm late; couldn't find anywhere to park. Have you been waiting long?'

'No,' he lies. He uses public transport and prides himself on his punctuality. But it's a Sunday and a Bank Holiday weekend, and he has enjoyed watching the passers-by while waiting for her.

They fall into step and conversation as they stroll towards the rose garden. A few yards into the garden, she stops to admire a yellow species, goes up close, inhales – something he has seen her do many times on the many walks they have made over the years. It's part of the pleasure of walking with her, her uninhibited expressions of enjoyment.

Sitting on a bench farther into the park, near a fountain with an elaborate sculpture, the Post Office Tower visible above the trees, sunlight bathing the garden in a gentle warmth, he is pleased to be in her company. She tells him about a recent long walk in the Pennines with a girlfriend. He tells her about a long walk he made on the Sussex Downs as a schoolboy. While recounting this distant episode in his life, he vaguely recalls having told her about it before, but her laughter, light and easy, doesn't betray any impatience at the retelling. He has listened to her repeat episodes from her past life, also.

Their day ends in the Brunswick Centre in Bloomsbury, at Carluccio's, an Italian eatery. They take a table outside. Night has arrived, and she is now wearing a shawl retrieved from her car. She has vegetable lasagne and a glass of white wine, he has pasta with prawns and a beer. They talk about the unusual architecture of the centre, its derelict years, its recent revival; speculate about the comfort of living in spaces with so much glass.

He remembers his days as a student at a nearby college and expresses regret that he had passed over opportunities to live in Central London. She chides him playfully for holding such a foolish thought.

'In my mid- fifties,' he says, 'my regrets are an important part of who I am.'

She laughs. 'I suppose, but having regrets seems like such a waste of emotional energy.'

'Are you saying you have no regrets?'

She thinks for a few seconds. 'I guess we all have a few regrets, don't we, if we're being honest.'

'I was trying to be honest, then,' he says. They both laugh. 'Can you name a regret?'

'Getting married to the first man I had sex with. We were far too young for marriage.' She pauses.

'It was the Christian thing to do,' he says. He knows about her childless marriage, her flight from its constraints in her early thirties, her ex-husband with whom she used to exchange birthday and Christmas cards.

'Are you still in touch, you and Jonathan?'

'No. I haven't seen him for several years. We used to meet once a year, as you know; then I started travelling. Sent him postcards. I was the one who made the effort to stay in touch, he was too busy with his career and family. Then I stopped. It seemed so pointless. There was nowhere to go in that relationship and I wanted to go forward. Marrying was certainly the Christian thing to do, but it wasn't the right thing, for me at least.'

He has never married, but he is a father, and he hears in her voice a strenuous effort to sound dispassionate, matter-of-fact, which is new. He maintains a sympathetic silence, which is broken when she enquires after his son, Chad.

'Oh, he's fine. I think. I haven't seen him for a few months. My troubled relationship with his mother is reflected in our relationship. I don't actually know how to improve matters; don't think there's much that I can do, except to be available when he wants to see me and to call him every so often. I messed up there big time.'

'From what I know, you tried. That's all you could have done in that situation.'

'Guess so.' He feels oddly comforted by her.

He releases a dry cough and feels better. She is the only person he can talk to about his offspring. Their past romantic mishaps, so different in outcomes, have always been a powerful bond between them, and this evening he feels especially close to her.

He feels tired when he gets home, but it's the pleasurable exhaustion of having passed time with an old friend, of being able to unburden himself, of sharing the intimate details of their past unhappy lives.

The following morning, he finds himself thinking about her: five years as lovers, then over a decade as friends. They never formally broke up, just drifted apart, after which she had lived abroad in several countries – France, America, Australia – bringing back small gifts for him. As he wanders through the day he notices these gifts: a piece of cloth with an Aboriginal design that is draped over an armchair, a candleholder made from amethyst crystals, a cigarette case, never used, that sits on a bookshelf. Why, he wonders, has he never noticed these gifts before?

He feels an overwhelming need to call and thank her for yesterday and all the days they have shared. He dials her number, but does not get an answer and there's no answering machine or service. He could try her mobile number, but reasons that if she's not at home, she must be busy. Besides, despite his agitation he's not actually sure he wants to talk to her. He seems to have seen a great deal of her in recent years. He tries a second time, then gives up.

The following day, she is still on his mind. He struggles to concentrate on his work but is unable to block her out. Memories come rushing back. One in particular replays between all the others.

It's early one Sunday afternoon and they have spent Saturday night together. They are in the kitchen of her flat and she is wearing an ankle-length, pale red floral dressing gown. Her hair is tousled, her cheeks flushed. She is making breakfast; later on they will probably make dinner together. He is sitting at the kitchen table beside the window and the sky is blue. From wall-mounted speakers comes the sound of a soprano singing in a foreign language. She comes and goes from the kitchen, her dressing gown flowing around her, and there is a delightful femininity about her every movement, an entrancing dance of womanliness that is as satisfying to watch as one of nature's wonders.

She calls that evening.

'You've been trying to get hold of me.'

'Yes, how did you know?' Hearing her voice calms him.

'I dialled 1471.'

'Oh. I just wanted to thank you for Sunday. I really enjoyed our time together.'

'Me, too,' she says.

'Are you doing anything this weekend?'

'Yes, I have a deadline on several cases for next Monday and I am due to have Sunday lunch with Karen. You remember Karen?'

'Yes, of course I remember Karen. Give her my regards.'

'Will do. My diary seems pretty full for the autumn. I'm doing two evening classes, and there are a couple of family events coming up.'

'Look. You've been on my mind quite a bit since Sunday.'

'Really? Why? I only saw you a month before last Sunday. What's happening?'

'I guess I have just been thinking about our relationship, you know, when we were together.'

'Oh.'

'I can't remember whether I ever told you how much I appreciated it, being with you. I was going through such a difficult phase in my life. Looking back, I think you gave me sanctuary, shelter. We didn't live together, but the time we shared was still a sort of sanctuary. The walks we took, the movies we saw, the dinners we shared; making love. Everything. Thank you.'

'No, you never told me. I am very pleased to hear that. Thank you.'

She sounds distant and he feels awkward and wants to end the conversation. 'What about the following weekend?'

'To meet up?'

'Yes.'

'I am booked up then, too, but that's not set in stone. Shall I give you a call if it falls free?'

'Okay. Yes. Do.'

'Will do. Must get on with my reports now.'

'Okay, bye.'

'Bye.'

He puts down the phone, breathes in deeply, and is filled with an inexplicable feeling of satisfaction. He sleeps soundly that night.

A week later, she calls to say her Sunday date has been cancelled. They agree to have dinner, then watch a movie. They meet at the Angel, Islington, on a warm evening. She has a new haircut, which makes her face seem slimmer, and wears pale pink lipstick.

Over the meal in a Turkish restaurant on Upper Street, she tells him about the past fortnight, the colleague at work who has been giving her a difficult time. He remembers this about her, she always seems to be locked in battle with one or other colleague. He listens attentively, his eyes drinking in the familiar features of her face under the restaurant's dim light. Noticing the crow's feet around her eyes, a thought crosses his mind: *she gave me the last years of her youth*. They met when she was thirty-eight and he was forty-four.

He finds the movie at the Screen on the Green unremarkable; she dismisses it as silly. They agree it was a disappointing effort by a once-great director.

The pavement is crowded and they struggle to remain walking side-by-side. Suddenly she says, 'Give me some fucking space. You're pushing me into the shop windows.'

He apologises and moves away; other pedestrians separate them. Her aggressive outburst unsettles him, makes him feel clumsy and awkward. He reminds himself that she has that side to her, what he used to call 'the bovver girl' in her. It's some minutes before he regains his equanimity; by then they have reached the Angel. He wants to ask her when they will meet again, but he senses she is keen to get away. They stand about talking for a few minutes, then hug affectionately and part.

The next morning, he finds himself not just thinking about her but craving her company with an uncontrollable intensity far worse than anything previously experienced. He is puzzled. Even at the height of their relationship, weeks and months often passed with there being no contact between them. Sometimes, not wishing to see her, he pleaded work pressure or feeling out of sorts or having to meet his son. He tells himself they were, at best, weekend lovers, two lonely people who met when it was mutually convenient.

But his memories defy him. He remembers, too, the night she telephoned at 10 p.m. to tell him she was entertaining Charlie Brewster, an acquaintance of his she had met through him, and he wished her and her guest a good evening. When he next saw her, he suggested she give him a key to her flat, something she herself had first mooted years before.

She refused, saying: 'You're jealous – and jealousy can't be a reason for moving in together.'

'I'm not saying we should move in together. Besides, you put me in an impossible position. If I don't react, you say I don't care; if I react, you say I'm jealous.'

'You have long known I am a person of contradictions. I still maintain that your jealousy isn't a good reason for giving you a key to my home.'

'You're right,' suddenly aware that she had played him and was pleased with the result, his jealousy. He wondered what would have happened if he had pressed her for a key in the earliest days, when their love was young and filled with hope. But he knew he had not asked for a key because having it implied a greater commitment than he was capable of making.

Now, years later, he cannot remember the sequence of events, for how much longer they remained lovers, when it was that their relationship transmuted into friendship. But the failure of his memory is less worrying than this raging desire to be in her presence. This craving is wrong, he tells himself repeatedly. Over ten years have passed, we have both moved on in our lives. He regains enough control to avoid calling her, but she continues floating just below the surface of his consciousness, sometimes demanding such attention that only long walks in his local park restore his balance.

Around the end of September he decides to make one last bid for peace from what he has now decided is an unhealthy preoccupation with her. He will buy her a present. Over the course of a week he spends his afternoons visiting jewellery stores and finally settles on a gold leaf brooch inset with sapphires. He is relieved when she agrees to meet and even more relieved that she likes the gift. And afterwards he does indeed enjoy a few days of peace, but the craving returns with renewed intensity.

He telephones her one Sunday in mid-October. She sounds pleased to hear his voice.

'I've been thinking about you,' he says. 'There's something I have to tell you.'

'Oh yeah?'

'Yes. I love you, I love you, I love you. I truly love you.' He is aware of himself uttering these simple words and is struck by their force and complexity. He hears her crying.

She stops, thanks him and says, 'I love you, too. You know that. But why do you feel the need to tell me you love me now?'

'Because I couldn't in the past, not properly. Put it down to some sort of blockage. But I am unblocked now. I love you.' He laughs joyfully until she speaks again.

'The problem is, though, I am in love with somebody else. You met him at my birthday party last year – Ajun Anwar.'

'I remember him. The maritime engineer. A pleasant man.'

He feels a tightening in his stomach and suddenly fears he has made a fool of himself with his rash declaration of love. But he quickly decides he has done something he needed to do, ought to have done years ago, and must accept its consequences.

'Are you happy with him?'

'No, we're not together. The relationship only lasted for six months, but dragged on for a few years. It ended two years ago. He wanted children, something I couldn't give him. He's working in Argentina now and is about to marry a woman twenty years his junior.'

'I'm sorry,' he says, needlessly. 'That's a tough one. Unrequited love.'

'Yeah. He really got under my skin. I felt I was myself with him, felt that I could allow him to see the real me.'

'You didn't feel that with me?'

'No. I often felt I had to be a little girl with you because that was the only way you would accept me.'

'That's not true. Well, I can't tell you how you felt. But I always saw you as a woman. Always.' Then he remembers once telling her that he preferred seeing her in her home because she always seemed so much more grown-up there.

'Maybe I exaggerate a bit, I mean about allowing you to treat me like a little girl.'

'No, no. I think there's some truth in that.' Now he remembers the dress she wore when they met in August, the little blue skirt she used to wear with black tights in the winter. Was she dressing for him on those occasions? Does she know him better than he knows himself? These questions make him feel uncomfortable and he wants to end the conversation.

'We all do that, don't we?' she says. 'Present different aspects of ourselves in order to get what we want.'

'And what did you want?'

'Your love.'

'And you didn't feel I loved you back then?'

'Yes and no. You loved the person I allowed you to see. Not the real me. Ajun, the man I am in love with but can't have, he saw the real me.'

'You can hardly blame me if you were dissembling. You didn't give me a chance to love the real you. Actually, now I think about it, if by the real you, you mean that aggressive and steely woman, I do know that person, too.'

'True. That's why I said I was exaggerating. Anyway, none of that matters much now. You need to know that I am thinking of joining a law firm in Marlborough.'

'You're leaving London?'

'Not immediately. If it happens, and it's looking increasingly likely that it will, I shall keep my London flat for a while. Rent out a room. Come and go.'

For a moment he feels as though she has lured him to a cliff edge and pushed him over and he is falling, but he catches himself and miraculously reverses his descent.

'I hope things work out,' he says.

'You don't care that I am leaving London?'

'I do, of course. But I love you and so must accept what you decide is best for you.'

'That's very adult.'

'I try,' he says, teetering on the brink again.

'Whatever happens I do hope we won't lose contact.'

'Me, too.'

They say goodbye, and he puts down the phone. He feels relieved for having told her he loves her and regrets he had not done so in the past. He floats through the rest of the day on a light cloud of vaguely sweet longing.

The following day, she's still on his mind. One moment he feels anger towards her, then the warmest tenderness. He thinks of going to stand outside her apartment building in the hope of seeing her, or writing her a long, passionate letter. His agitated ambivalence continues into the afternoon, so he decides to go for a walk. His perambulation takes him into Dalston and there, as he is passing a travel agent he sees a sign: *Low Fares to Spain.*

Damn it, he thinks, I need to get out of here, get away for a while. I have the savings. He goes in and books a ten-day trip for the end of the following week.

That weekend, on a Sunday morning, over the telephone he tells her of his travel plans.

'That's sudden,' she says.

'Decided on a whim. Really. It would be lovely to see you before I go. Maybe we could go for a walk in the park today. Have an early dinner somewhere.'

'I'm feeling a bit rundown,' she says. 'I just need to stay home and rest.'

'I could come over with the Sunday papers. We can hang out together for the day.'

'That's a nice idea. But I need to learn to spend more time by myself. You told me that once, do you remember?'

'Yes, but that was years ago. I also remember telling you at the time that it would be nice to be in the same space with you without having to always interact with you. That was part of the problem in the past. We only met to play. And if we weren't fucking each other or talking, we couldn't be together.'

'Maybe. But I was hurt by what you said back then.'

'So now you're trying to hurt me?'

'No. Not at all. But I thought about it a great deal over the years, and decided that you were right. I'd like to be as self-contained as you.'

'As I used to be. We all change.' He senses that she would like him to plead for her company, as she used to do for his in the past. He lacks her powers of persuasion. He settles instead for a long telephone conversation. Putting down the phone, he mutters to himself, 'We missed the moment and can't revive it. I must get away.'

They talk again on the eve of his departure.

'You haven't travelled for a while,' she says. 'I hope you go away for a long time.'

'You don't care that I'm going away?'

'I am hardly the person to discourage anyone from travelling. What time is your flight?'

'Three-thirty. Gatwick.'

'I hope you have a great time.'

'Thanks.'

On an overcast autumn day he arrives in Gatwick, checks in his luggage then wanders outside for a cigarette. Back inside the terminus, he buys a newspaper and a paperback book. He doesn't want to go through the departures gate as yet; wants to delay the moment when he has to divest himself of objects essential to his feeling of security – keys, belt, shoes – in order to satisfy a greater security.

He takes a seat and looks at the hustle and bustle of the passengers. Then he recalls to himself various films in which lovers, separated by misunderstanding, are finally and joyfully reunited at an airport or railway station. He feels compelled to search for a familiar face among the passengers but doesn't see her face. A wave of sadness combining longing and loneliness courses through him, lifts him out of his seat and sweeps him to the departures gate. The female attendant takes his passport, rifles through it, returns it. Passport in hand, he advances a step then glances back one last time.

After passing through security, he goes straight to a bar and orders a whisky on the rocks. His first sip arouses in him a craving for nicotine that supersedes his previous craving. He forces himself to sit still, as still as possible, and in the stillness feels a gentle warmth from the whisky, and it occurs to him that he's now a free man, a man free to love again.

Turning White

Early autumn. Reece was on his way to the barbershop on Sandringham Road. He walked along Brighton Drive, which had a deserted air about it at this hour, nearing midday. People were at work; children in school. He had always liked this street of terraced houses. Many had been lovingly restored, their sash windows and doors with stained-glass panels too pristine to be original. He saw a woman, white and middle-aged, her steps jaunty, walking towards him on the same side of the street. She must have noticed him at the same time because she immediately crossed the road.

The woman's action was a jolting reminder to Reece that, though he held down a respectable job in the Borough Council's Planning Department, had never had any contact with the police except for a minor driving offence, had gone straight from school to university, to some people in some spaces he was a young black male, a dangerous and feral urban creature. Then: Stop being paranoid, Reece thought. She was probably planning to cross the road anyway.

His gaze fell on a rowan tree, its berries squashed on the pavement, then an overgrown hedge. He returned his attention to admiring the houses on Brighton Drive.

Twenty minutes later, he was sitting in the barber's chair. He was the only customer.

Warwick, the proprietor and main barber, draped the red plastic cape around his customer's neck. Warwick's colleague, Luther, was seated two chairs away reading the *Daily Mirror*.

Reece watched the reflection of Warwick's tall, lumbering figure reach for the shears.

'Usual?' Warwick said.

'Yes.'

He felt the afro-pick pass through his hair in an upward motion, and wondered how long Warwick had been a barber, and what made a man choose that line of work.

'Your hair's thinning fast, Reece,' Warwick said. 'Remember when passing a comb through your hair was like passing it through steel wool?'

'Still feels thick to me,' Reece said. He was only thirty-two. He glanced at the reflection of Warwick's small dark afro, which framed a brown face with full, pendulous cheeks. There were a few strands of white, but Warwick's hair was luxuriantly thick and glossy.

'Definitely thinning and thinning fast; a few white hairs, too,' Warwick said, his rumbling voice as grave as a doctor's delivering an unfavourable prognosis to a patient.

'Let me see,' Luther said.

Reece saw Luther rise from the chair. Luther was much younger than Warwick. He was small with a matt black complexion, high cheekbones and a dimple in his clean-shaven chin; his own hair was cut low with sharp lines at the front and sides, which made it seem as though he was wearing a sort of skullcap. Warwick stepped back as Luther scrutinised Reece's hair.

'Warwick's right, you know. Receding, too. Better take care or it'll be gone in a few years.'

'That's depressing news,' Reece said.

'Make sure you oil it every day; slows down the thinning. Not much you can do about the receding hairline – luck of the draw,' Warwick said.

'Could try shaving off the whole thing for a while, oil the scalp daily – any good quality oil, olive, argan – that works for some people,' Luther said, back behind his newspaper.

Reece saw Warwick give a respectful nod, as if impressed by his colleague's tonsorial knowledge.

'What about the white hairs?' Reece asked.

'Nothing to worry about. Can always dye that,' Warwick said.

'Like Warwick,' Luther said from behind his newspaper.

'Got to keep the ladies looking,' Warwick said.

'Ladies! Come on, Warwick, you've been married for almost forty years.'

'Exactly. Nothing like a bit of a competition to keep your lady loyal.'

'I'll remember that when I give a speech at your next wedding anniversary.'

Warwick laughed as he switched on the razor, ending his badinage with his colleague to better concentrate on the job at hand.

Reece left the barbershop and walked out to Stoke Newington High Street. He didn't give much thought to the barbers' comments on his hair. But as he passed Ozcan Turkish Patisserie, he caught sight of his reflection in the window and was suddenly alarmed by what he saw. They were right: with the sunlight on his head, his scalp was almost visible.

From that day, Reece began to wage a war against his thinning hair. His bathroom shelf groaned with the weight of hair products that promised to promote hair growth: carrot and olive oil, Morgan's Pomade, Dax Pomade with bergamot, avocado and mango shampoo. In his preparation for work, he factored in an extra fifteen minutes to daily massage his scalp, and repeated the exercise again at night. When, on his next visit to the barber, he once again heard Warwick's negative comments on his thinning hair, he decided on a course of extreme action: he decided to shave his head.

For this purpose, and to save the expense of frequent visits to the barber, he bought a set of electric razors, which came with an attachment for nose and ear hair. A few of his colleagues made favourable comments on his new appearance, and any remaining doubts he had were vanquished when he started a relationship with Laura Sturgess, an architect. Months later, she was superseded by June Wickham, an estate agent, who took perverse pleasure in stroking his bald head in a gesture of post-coital tenderness. Many others followed, too many to mention.

Some years later, in spring, Reece contracted a severe bout of flu and was bedridden for a week. Like many people who enjoy robust good health, illness made him depressed, a condition exacerbated by the recent demise of a relationship in which he had invested great hope. On the first morning that he felt strong enough to resume his shaving routine, he looked in the mirror and what he saw startled him. The hair on top of his head was not only wispy, it was white, as was his seven-day stubble. He forced himself to continue looking at his reflection, and the longer he looked the less this metamorphosis alarmed him. His facial features did not seem any older - there were no creases in his forehead and no visible laughter lines.

He could not bring himself to shave, so decided to visit his barber on Sandringham Road. The twenty-minute walk would do him good.

He stopped in the corner shop for a packet of cigarettes, and some mints. On giving him his change, the shopkeeper, a Turkish man with a narrow face and jet-black hair who had recently taken over the shop, said, 'Thank you, sir.' It was only when he got outside that the shopkeeper's politeness registered on Reece. Needs to keep his customers, he thought.

He cut through Butterfield Green, the small park in Stoke Newington, walked along Wordsworth Road, then Matthias Road. From the Rio Cinema, he crossed over into Sandringham Road. But his journey had been futile: the barbershop was no longer there. Reece stood in front of the boarded-up shop and tried to remember when he had last visited it. Must be at least three years, he decided. Disappointed, he walked back to Stoke Newington High

Street and headed in the general direction of home, wondering what had happened to Warwick.

At a Turkish café near Palatine Road he stopped and had a coffee, choosing to sit at an outside table so he could smoke. It was many years since he had taken much notice of this part of the borough. The Turkish-owned establishments – cafés, convenience stores, jewellery stores, kebab joints – had grown exponentially.

He finished his coffee, went inside to pay, and the young man took his money, handed him his change and said, 'Thank you, sir'. He left a generous tip.

He chose the route down Brighton Drive to get home. The houses near the main road were, he saw, neglected, with faded paint on their doors and window frames, but they soon gave way to houses that were better maintained. Midway down Brighton Drive, he noticed a woman walking towards him on the same side of the pavement. She was white and elderly and walked with confident steps. Then a particularly attractive row of houses – their brickwork recently pointed, their doors and window frames freshly painted, their gardens immaculately kept – caught his eye and he no longer noticed the woman approaching until she was a few steps from him at a point where a rowan tree narrowed the width of the pavement. He stopped and stood aside, allowing her to pass, and thought he heard her whisper a 'Thank you.'

The Dinner Lady

You really want to know how I came to be here, here in this white and grey room in Dalston on a black and grey autumn day, listening to a man telling me how to apply for a job, how to fill in an application form, how to dress, how to conduct myself at an interview, I, who was born on Morning Lane and grew up on the Hackney Downs estate – yes, the same one where they rioted a few years back; wouldn't have happened in my days, not in my days, we knew how to behave then – me, a woman approaching fifty, a mother and grandmother, me, who used to work for the PO, and in the Park Lane Hilton, me, who used to be in charge of feeding over a thousand children for five days a week for most of the year – you really want to know how I came to be in this job club?

OK. I'll tell you, Babes.

It's like this, Babes. See, in my last job, about two years back, I was in charge, had six, seven people working for me, had to plan all the school meals. Not a major complaint in four years. Kids were happy. My staff was happy. Inspector said I kept a kitchen that was an example of excellent hygiene. *Excellent hygiene.* His words, not mine. Where? You know Gresham Grove School, secondary? Yes, that one, Babes. I was The Dinner Lady, yes, me. If I didn't do my job right, kids couldn't concentrate on their afternoon classes. I mean, you can't think about equilateral triangles, or Henry the Eighth, or Shakespeare if your stomach is empty or you have the runs. You know what I mean, Babes?

So, one day we had a vacancy. I ended up taking on a girl in her twenties, Deborah. Mixed. She wasn't my favourite. Couldn't say why. I mean, she was well turned out, her shoes were clean, her clothes pressed, she didn't wear a whole heap of make-up or a whole heap of bling. And you might think this a little strange, but you know how some people have a thing about teeth, other people a thing about eyes, for some people it's hands ... well, I have a thing about ears, clean ears, and no dangling earrings because in my books a woman who wears dangling earrings is advertising herself for sale. Look at that Rihanna; nuff said. Know what I mean, Babes?

Anyway, this Deborah, her ears were very clean and she wore simple round earrings. Nothing more than nine-carat gold – I can tell these things. And yet I didn't feel quite right about her. Just gut instincts, or as my mother used to say, 'my spirit never really took to her.' In fact, if my mother had still been alive it was just the sort of thing I'd have talked about to her on the phone. We used to talk two or three times day. I never made a major decision without talking things through with her, like whether I should take the job as a dinner lady. She said yes, so I did. Three years later she was gone. Heart attack. Still miss her. Excuse me, can't mention her without my eyes getting wet ... That's better. Used to get through a lot of hankies. Not so bad now.

So, my mother wasn't around, and in any case, my team members all liked this Deborah. You've got to keep your team happy. One said she knew the mother, Jewish, from up Stamford Hill – you know, where all those Hata ... What you say? Hasidic, that's it, Hasidic Jews. Can you imagine that? And the father a mystery – African, though. Her surname was African, you see. Made me wonder, I can tell you, but my main concern was the job, and my team liked her. So I hired her.

Babes, let me tell you, it was one of the biggest mistakes of my life.

She was all right for the first term. Autumn. Punctual. That's another thing I am very fussy about. If I say nine o'clock, I mean nine o'clock, not five or even three minutes past. Better you arrive early and wait otherwise you might just find a locked gate. You like that, Babes? It's one of Paul's lines. Who's Paul? My man, of course. We've been together for twenty-eight years now. Two children. Never married. Said we didn't need a preacher to tell us about love. It's true, you know. Look at me and Paul. Mind you, I had to train him, especially about this time thing. But when he came home late for dinner a few times and found that I'd ate mine and thrown his share in the bin, he learned how serious I was about punc-tu-aa-litee.

Now, where was I? Yes, she was all right at first. A bit slow on the uptake, but I couldn't complain. Then one Monday morning she turned up at work and announced that she had become a Muslim. I remember that morning well because I was trying out a new hairstyle and it was my first day at work with it. I didn't really know what to say at first. There she was in a long black skirt, black top, her head covered in a black headscarf. I mean, I was stunned. Stunned into silence. When I recovered I said, 'I don't care who or where you worship as long as you do the job you were employed to do.' And that was it as far as I was concerned.

A month later, one of the team, Shalika – a good worker, solid team member – started complaining that Jamilla – yes, that's what she wanted us to call her now – wasn't pulling her weight. How she was always taking time out to pray. Had a spot in the store-room where she would roll out her mat, always facing east, and pray to Allah.

Well, I had to talk to her about that, Jamilla or Deborah, that is. Couldn't let that pass, hear what I am saying, Babes? No.

Called her into my office the next day. Told her how it was. The time allowed for tea breaks, lunch and so on. How our whole working day was about making sure those hungry children got fed. She listened, then you know what she said? You wouldn't believe what she said! 'You're just anti-Muslims.' Gordon bleeding Bennett! I couldn't believe my ears. Me, born on Morning Lane and raised on Hackney Downs estate, me, with a brother who's Rastafarian and two older sisters who spend so much time at that Trinitarian church on ... what's the name of that road – oh, you know where ... so much time they can't find men, me, whose parents used to tell us about race prejudice when they first came to England, you know, all that no dogs, no Irish, no blacks nonsense – *me* anti-Muslims?

I give her one look, you see, and I say, 'Girl, you trying it on?' She had to look away. Had to. Anyway, she left my office after saying that she didn't know that her praying was taking too much time out of her work and she would do better.

And she did for a while. Then things just started getting worse. Her mid-morning prayer could last as long as thirty minutes. Can you imagine that, when we had all that preparation to do to feed those hungry children? And you got to know that for some of them, school dinner is the most balanced meal of the day, healthier than all that rubbish some parents give their children – if they can afford to buy food, that is. Remember, we're in Hackney. Well, Babes, I had to put my foot down. The whole team was complaining.

I had another little talk with her. And another. But no matter how much I talked, she was just behaving the same, long prayer sessions mid-morning, and afternoon, when we have to clean the kitchen. Then one day, we had bangers and mash, pork sausages. The child said she couldn't touch pork.

'Nobody is asking you to eat pork,' I told her. 'Just serve it to the kids.'

'I can't, my religion forbids it,' she insisted.

That was the last straw for me. It wasn't the first time we had served pork since she started the job. I dismissed her on the spot. Told her to leave the school premises until Friday, when she could come back for her wages. It seemed like the best thing to do at the time, especially because the following day I heard from one of the team how this Jamilla had earlier in the week bent her ears about the loose morals of the girls in the school, their short skirts and tight blouses and all that, and how she, Jamilla, always served such girls with a scowling expression.

Now, I ask you. This is London, isn't it? I mean, I don't wear short skirts, but when I was a teenager I liked showing off my legs. Which young girl doesn't? And I had a fine pair of legs – still do; used to get a whole heap of compliments 'bout my legs, from girls, too. Sometimes Paul even complains that I only wear trousers and long skirts and how he misses seeing me in a skirt above the knees. But I just put him in his place and tell him I don't dress for no man, not even him. Know what I mean, Babes? So that girl was well out of order. Mind you, I heard that she did it – became a Muslim, that is – to get a certain man. Yes, Babes, to get a man. Cover herself from head to toe to get that man. Must be a sheikh or something like that. Would never get me dressing for a man, Babes, not me. Not for all the oil in Arabia.

Now listen to this. Two weeks after I sacked her – by the way, I found a replacement in no time; older woman, no chance of her pulling any nasty surprises like converting to Scientology or something like that – I only received notice that Jamilla was taking the school to court for unfair dismissal. Imagine that. Unfair dismissal! The union official come quizzing me, talking 'bout procedures and religious discrimination. Religious discrimination! What about all those schools that only employ you if you belong to their faith? I know because I went for vacancies in a few of them. Couldn't get a foot in the door because I ain't a churchgoer.

Well, I told him it was my kitchen, and my business to see that it was run properly so the kids could get their lunch every day, and that that girl wasn't pulling her weight and that's why I fired her. So, anyway, things went to a tribunal. What a strain. Thank goodness for Paul – that man is a rock in my life. Girl got compensation. That's when I decided to find something else to do. I mean, I can cook for hundreds, parties, naming ceremonies, engagements, weddings – might even join a church 'cause they're always celebrating something or another. So that's what I am planning to do next. Start my own business. I mean, if I can't say who can work in my kitchen, and how they should work, what's the point?

Know what I mean, Babes?

Nights at COAC

The garden party had started around mid-afternoon, and at 8.30 p.m. on this hot July evening it showed no sign of ending any time soon.

From his third-floor kitchen window, through Venetian blinds, Ralph looked down at the neighbouring back garden teeming with teenagers celebrating the end of their school years. They sat on the walls, rolled about on a trampoline and, under a pavilion-shaped tent specially erected for the occasion, danced to reggae and hip-hop music. Ralph's closed windows and doors muted the noise but created another source of discomfort: a suffocating heat, which was at its worst in the low-ceilinged top-floor bedroom, also the farthest point in his home from the party. He had already taken a long walk around Clissold Park to escape the noise. The fresh air and open green space had strengthened his forbearance, but within a few hours of returning home, he had started to wilt again. Now, obeying a renewed urge to leave the house once more, he gathered his keys and ventured outside. The sight of three teenaged girls, latecomers, entering the house next door vindicated his decision: only nightfall and angry neighbours would restore his home to him.

His aimless wandering through the back streets brought him to Newington Green, where he paused to watch the setting sun bleeding through a thin layer of clouds above the colonnade of old plane trees. He left the Green and turned down Mildmay Grove, where, walking in the shadow of four-storey houses, he was reminded of the home he had been forced to temporarily abandon because a teenager had decided that midweek was an appropriate time for an end-of-school party. He tried to remember whether his own youth had been marked by such flagrant inconsideration of the rhythm of the adult week. Memories rushed forward like volunteers for a good cause.

Lost in thought, he became aware of his surroundings again when he reached Gillett Square. He stopped to look at the notices in the window of the Vortex nightclub: a jazz trio was performing that night. He entered the square and went into the bar below the Vortex. He ordered a pint of lager and took it back outside. All the tables were occupied, but there was an upended steel beer keg in a corner. He sat there and took a draught from the glass of lager; the cold liquid coursing down his throat caused a pleasant shiver.

The square flowed and throbbed with life: at the far end, on the wooden stage under the pine trees, men sat in disparate groups; to the left of the stage there was a single large gathering of other men. To Ralph's right, on another elevation, men sat on chairs outside kiosks selling Nigerian food, Ethiopian coffee, Jamaican jerk chicken. One kiosk served as a computer repair workshop, another

was used for international money transfers. Outside the
nearest kiosk was a group of East Africans, Somalians,
maybe. The oldest man was reading what seemed like
a miniaturised copy of the Koran, and two young men
appeared to be bargaining over a wrap of khat. The sign
behind them on the kiosk read *Home Away from Away*.

A middle-aged English couple sat on the steps leading
to the kiosks while a boy, who looked like he might have
been the man's son, stood astride his bicycle. Near the
stage under a pine tree a young couple – she was black,
he was white; their bodies had a starved leanness – were
exhibiting their youth and love with long, lingering kisses.
From above and behind them came the sound of live jazz,
a screeching horn, guitar licks, the percussive thud of a
piano, the pianist playing his instrument like a drum,
pounding out chords and arpeggios.

The lager was beginning to make Ralph feel light-headed.
I'm drinking too fast, he thought. The party will probably
continue until ten; certainly no later than eleven. There's
still over an hour to kill. Minimum. Don't want to return
home drunk. This lager's not cheap, either. Slow down.

The sudden arrival of a group of skateboarders drew
his attention back to the square. Three teenage boys,
all white, were suddenly whizzing about at a dizzying
speed, the clanking sounds of their skateboard wheels
and wooden platforms on the stone surface adding a new
percussive sound, enriching the aural ambience. They
used the edge of the stage for practising leaps and flipping
their boards. An older boy joined them for a moment –
he sped diagonally across the square.

The other people in the square appeared serenely oblivious to the presence of the skateboarders; the conversations and surreptitious exchanges continued. The white middle-aged couple got up and left, with the boy on the bicycle riding slowly beside them.

He was wondering what it must be like to live in the apartments on the far side of the square beyond the car park, when he noticed her approaching. She was dressed entirely in black, black blouse and black jeans, with her jet-black hair pinned behind her head, strands falling about her swarthy face. Italian? Greek? Spanish? Portuguese? He couldn't tell. Kohl highlighted her eyes, her lips were a natural pale pink. She smiled at him and walked past him, stirring the warm air and leaving behind the disturbing scent of an elusive memory. He returned his attention to the square.

The long-drawn-out dusk was coming to a close. The temperature had dropped and his exposed arm felt cool, but not uncomfortably so. The skateboarders drifted away as the darkness, relieved by the electric light, settled over the square. There was now a vacant table outside the bar. He claimed it and from this new position he could see out to Kingsland Road, to the traffic moving slowly past. The lager, the warm night air, the buzz of conversations emanating from the now shadowy groups of figures, the discordant sound of music intermittently audible through the closed windows of the Vortex ... he was glad to be outside.

'Is this seat taken?' he heard. He looked up and saw the woman who had walked past him minutes before. Her beauty registered on him.

'No,' he said.

She placed a glass of red wine on the table, sat down and began to light a cigarette. He snatched glances at her, decided that she was older than he had first thought: at least mid- thirties.

'Is it always like this?' she asked.

'Filled with people?'

'Yes. And so many different kinds of people?'

'I don't really know,' he said. He thought he heard a slight trace of Spanish in her accent.

'*Español*?' he tried.

'*Sí, hablo Español*?'

He laughed and said, '*Pequito*. Words. Phrases. A few lines from Neruda.'

'You know Pablo Neruda's work?' She seemed suddenly animated.

'*Nació la palabra en la sangre* ... I can't remember the rest.'

'*Creció en el cuerpo oscuro, palpitando* ...'

'Yes, now I remember: *y voló con los* ...' He hesitated

'... *labios y la boca*,' she recited.

They laughed together.

'Neruda's "The Word" – the opening stanza. I'm afraid that's all I remember. It's quite a long poem.'

'I know the whole poem,' she said.

'You must have a pretty good memory.'

'And you must be a man of good taste to know Neruda.'

'It would be a slight exaggeration to say I know Neruda.'

'I mean his work.'

'That's what I mean, also. Where are you from?'

'That's not an easy question to answer.'

'Where were you born?'

'Venezuela.'

'You're a long way from home, then.'

'Home? It's just where my parents happened to be when I came into the world. I've lived in so many different countries, I don't know where home is. And you?'

'Jamaica. Sort of. But I've also lived in many countries.'

'If Venezuela is my home we're almost neighbours.'

'I suppose so, which is why I'm ashamed I'm only fluent in English, and even that I often struggle with.'

'I'm sure that's not true. Besides, you seem, how shall I say? Like someone who would fit in anywhere because you are so self-contained? There's stillness in your voice.'

'I take that as a compliment, thank you.'

'*De nada.*'

They fell silent and the sound of conversations elsewhere in the square came to his ears, with snatches of jazz from above. And in the pause in their own conversation, it occurred to Ralph that perhaps his youthful years of travelling had left him with an unwanted aura of universality. If that was the case, far from complimenting him, perhaps she had identified the problem plaguing his life: he longed to be here, in this city, London, nowhere else, and certainly not everywhere. In his ambition to achieve a quality of here-ness and fixity, he was failing.

She lit another cigarette, and he now felt something comforting about her presence. He thought of home. The party would be almost over, but he was reluctant to leave just yet.

'Can I buy you a drink?' he asked.

'Yes, thank you. Casa Sangre.' She pointed to her almost empty glass of red wine.

He returned with a glass of red wine, and a glass of scotch with ice for himself. Their glasses clinked, they said cheers, and with his first sip he told himself he would head home as soon as he finished his drink.

But they were still talking when the performance in the Vortex ended and the crowd in the square had thinned, leaving just a few groups of people, their voices coming to him in whispers borne on a gentle nocturnal breeze like the susurrations of trees. She had told him her name was Maria, and he had sipped his drink slowly and listened to her story about a peripatetic childhood driven by her businessman father and pliant mother, whose skill as an English language teacher often rescued the family from the father's failed business ventures. For now she worked as a waitress but sometimes a friend got her work as a film extra, which paid much better.

'I must be going, Maria,' he said at last. Summoning these few words required stupendous willpower, and even greater energy to utter because what he most desired was to sit with her on this warm night, at this table, watching the square empty, and maybe the sky would clear enough for them to make out the stars and the constellations.

'Me, too,' she said.

'Can I walk you to a bus stop, to the station?'

'No. I live just round the corner.'

'Can I walk you round the corner, then?' he said.

'Thank you.'

They left the square, passing the entrance to the Vortex, where the musicians were packing their instruments into a van. He was aware of her physical closeness to him, their synchronised steps. He felt desire stir in him.

A few minutes later he was in her top-floor room in a house beside the railway bridge. It was a small room, painted a pale green, and it smelled of oranges. A low single bed was beside the outer wall, under the window covered by a hanging cane blind. A black and red quilt was spread over the bed. Above the bed-head were two bookshelves, orderly and filled, as far as he could make out, with paperback editions of poetry collections: Neruda, Rimbaud, Wordsworth, Tennyson, Shakespeare, Whitman and other names he did not recognise.

On one wall, beside a dwarf wardrobe, was an unframed medium-sized print of Salvador Dali's *The Last Supper*, and on another wall a Frieda Kahlo self-portrait. There was an air of impermanence, of transience about the room, and he thought of his student digs from many years before.

'Nice room,' he said, for want of something to say.

'It's my home for now,' she said.

She was sitting on the bed, her back to the window, her legs stretched out on the floor, an elongated white bedside lamp switched on and turned up to the bookshelves. He went and sat beside her, and looked into her eyes. He placed his right hand on her neck and gently pulled her towards him. And as he expected she yielded, and they kissed long and deep with what he sensed was a mutual hunger.

Then she pulled away, her dark eyes searching his face, and said, 'Ralph, I don't want us to have sex. Not tonight. But I would like you to stay, stay as long as you like, and if I am sleeping when you decide to leave, leave quietly, please.'

All the tension of expectation and desire within him dissipated and he resiled at this surprising turn to the evening. A sudden laughter, awkward and anxious, erupted in him and spilled out. He said, 'Are you serious?'

'Yes, I am.' Her voice, almost a whisper, carried notes of sincerity and appeal.

'And what will we do if I stay?'

'Sleep,' she said, touching his shoulder. 'For the last two nights I have dreamt the same dream: I am sitting in an old leather armchair, an armchair like something from the nineteen-thirties, all creased and worn by time and bodies, and the armchair is in an oak-panelled room and rain is falling in this room, rain is falling steadily. Then the room fills with water and the armchair I am sitting in floats out of the window and along a wide avenue where all the houses are submerged. Only their chimney pots are visible on the surface of this flowing water ...'

'Sounds weird,' he interrupted.

'Yet I felt safe in that old armchair.'

'Then what happened?'

'The street of water flowing like a river became a lake, tranquil and blue, then the lake became a sea with waves so high I could touch the moon; and next I was plunging over the edge of the sea into darkness, as if plunging over the edge of the world. Then I was afraid and woke up. I don't want to have that dream again and if I do, I don't want to wake up alone.'

'So, you picked me up in a bar to spend the night with you?'

'Yes. I saw you and said to myself, "He does not look like a man who is afraid to dream."' She corrected herself. 'I mean, afraid of dreams.'

He passed his hand across his forehead in a theatrical gesture of despair and exasperation. Trust me, he thought. A crank. Loco.

'I'm no dream interpreter,' he said. 'A psychoanalyst would probably have great fun trying to interpret it for you.'

'Psychoanalysis! Quackery,' she scoffed. She fell silent, took off her shoes, manoeuvred herself onto the bed, and stretched out against the wall, her back to him.

He thought of his own bed, king-sized and comfortable, but felt no desire to leave. He removed his trainers and stretched out beside her, pressing into her to fit onto the bed. He placed an arm around her shoulder, and she raised her torso slightly so he could fit the other arm around her waist.

'Thank you,' she said.

'*De nada.*'

He lay awake for some minutes thinking about this strange anti-climax to the evening, and what sort of woman invited a stranger into her bed for the sole purpose of actually just sleeping, and what kind of stranger accepted such an invitation; then he remembered lonely nights when he, too, would have risked his life in the comforting arms of a stranger – and with that memory her request seemed less odd.

Next, he heard a rumbling metallic sound; the bed shook and the window rattled. He must have fallen asleep. Now awake, he remembered that he was in a house beside a railway line. A passing freight train had woken him up. When his eyes adjusted to the darkness, he saw that somehow, in that brief period of sleep, they had turned round. Her face was now buried in the back of his neck; one of her arms was above his head and another under his left arm and across his chest.

He looked at his watch and saw that it was 1.35 a.m. He had slept for two hours but felt fully rested, as if he had slept all night.

'You're leaving,' he heard her say.

'Yes, I'd better go,' he said. He extricated himself from her arms and sat on the edge of the bed, putting on his trainers. She rose up behind him and embraced him, her chin on his right shoulder, her breath warm and vaguely minty.

'Don't go,' she said.

'It's quite late, heading to two o'clock.'

'That's not late. Let's go to COAC.'

'COAC?'

'Yes, COAC.' She spelled out the word. 'You don't know COAC, the all-night café? They sometimes have music. Acoustic only.'

He got up from the bed and stretched his arms in the air, almost touching the ceiling.

'I'll dress for you,' she said. She was kneeling on the bed and he noticed now that her eyes were naturally large, her pupils black, and there was the hint of the Native American in her ovoid and flat face.

'You'll what?' he laughed.

'Dress for you. Dress just for you.'

'How do you know what I like?'

'So you'll come if I dress for you?'

'Hold on, I didn't say that.'

It was her turn to laugh and she did so with gusto and a note of such playfulness that he conceded defeat. He returned to sitting on the bed.

She kissed him on his cheek, got off the bed and opened the wardrobe. Using the wardrobe door as a screen she began to change her clothes, humming as she went about this exercise. He saw her pale ankles and feet with the toenails painted green and, floating above the wardrobe door, her darker neck and face, framed by black, stylishly unkempt hair.

'*Voila!*' she said, stepping away from the wardrobe. She was now wearing a blue sleeveless lace dress, which flared at the waist and stopped just below her knees.

He coughed in an effort to conceal his surprise at how pleasing she looked. He complimented her on her sartorial taste.

'Actually, this dress was my mother's. It fits perfectly now – it didn't always, as for many years it was too large. But I haven't quite finished.'

She stepped back behind the wardrobe door and he guessed she was putting on tights; then he saw her kneel down to tie the laces of pointed, low-heeled brown shoes with a brogue pattern.

They strolled out into the warm night air, entered the square from Bradbury Street and turned left onto Kingsland Road. There were still many people around at this hour; they milled about outside basement nightclubs where muscular bouncers guarded the doors. As the couple walked, they talked.

'Are you in the habit of inviting complete strangers to your room?' he asked.

'Only if they can recite Neruda,' she said.

'Just a line?'

'No, I am usually more demanding. An entire poem. But for you I made an exception.' She laughed and they walked on in silence.

He had known her for only a few hours and yet he felt entirely at ease with her and had no doubt that she felt the same. When they turned into Shacklewell Lane, he asked her what had brought her to London, and while concentrating on listening to her answer he paid no attention to where they were going. She told him she had been a student at the Courtauld Institute for six months when her father's talent for business failure reached its spectacular climax, resulting in him committing suicide. She had withdrawn from the Courtauld, gone to live with her mother in Miami, Florida, for a while, and then returned to Europe, living in Paris, Madrid, Berlin, Milan and Marseilles before coming back to London.

'And will you stay in London? I mean, settle here?'

'It depends.'

'On what?'

'I don't know,' she said. '*Que sera, sera.*'

'Isn't that a rather fatalistic attitude?'

'How do you mean?'

'Surely, life's what you make of it. You know, agency and all that?'

'Agency?'

'Purpose, goals, action. We exercise choice and act.'

'I chose to talk to you, didn't I? I initiated a conversation; I invited you into my home. Isn't that agency?'

'True.'

She touched his arm and said, 'Here we are, COAC.'

They were in a cobbled mews outside a warehouse building with a double blue door, wide and high enough for a Transit van to drive in. A regular-sized door was embedded in the left panel, and there was a vertical column of bell buttons on the wall. She pressed one of the bells, the smaller door opened and they stepped into what seemed like a courtyard centred on an island of plants until Ralph looked up and saw that they had entered an atrium. Customers were sitting at tables to the left of the atrium and on the right was a counter.

They ordered two herbal teas – camomile for her, rooibos for him – and drifted to the rear of the building, where they took a table. In the farthest corner, on a small, dimly lit stage, a bearded man strummed a guitar but the music was barely audible. Ralph had noticed people playing chess and reading at some tables in the atrium, and here he saw other chess players, along with card players, and if he was not mistaken there was a game of Scrabble being played at one table between three people.

'I didn't know about this place,' Ralph said, 'and I have lived in Hackney for years.'

'You do now. Welcome to COAC.'

They resumed their conversation, ordered more tea, and for a few minutes listened to the guitar player who wasn't singing but humming as he strummed his guitar in a style of music that defied Ralph's limited musical knowledge but which he found pleasing. For a disconcerting moment Ralph thought they were being watched by a man sitting at a table on the other side of the room. The light was dimmer there, the man's face was hidden, but he could make out his fedora and red brocaded waistcoat below a striped cream jacket. But it was just his imagination, he decided.

Leaving the café, they stepped into a bright morning with a pale blue sky and the sun rising above the buildings behind them. A few yards from the café, she placed her right arm in the crook of his left arm and said, 'Sorry, COAC was a bit quiet tonight. It's quite lively sometimes.'

'Oh, don't apologise, I liked it.'

They walked on in silence through several back streets, which Ralph did not recognise because he seldom came to this part of the borough. But he knew exactly where he was when they emerged on to Stoke Newington High Street and he saw the police station to his left on the other side of the street.

'Well, that was an adventure,' he said.

'We must do it again,' she said.

'What are you going to do with the rest of the day?'
Ralph asked.

'What would you like me to do?'

'Come home with me.'

After two days in Ralph's place, most of which they spent
in bed, she left saying she had to do a week's shift at the
West End restaurant where she worked. Ralph walked her
to her home.

Over the next week Ralph tried to concentrate on his
search for work. One night, around 2 a.m., he was woken
from his sleep by the sound of his doorbell ringing. He
looked out of the top-floor bedroom window and saw her
standing below the street light on the opposite side of the
street. He went downstairs, opened the front door, but
there was nobody there. The street was empty. He went
back to bed and when he woke up the next morning, he
wasn't sure whether the incident in the night had been a
dream.

The week passed and when he didn't hear from her he
went to the house near Gillett Square and only then did
he notice that the door had neither a bell nor a knocker.
He thought for a moment, then decided to shout through
the letterbox, though he knew she lived on the top floor
in a rear room and was unlikely to hear him even if she
was home. He returned home disappointed but confident
that she would eventually make contact because he was
sure that they had bonded that night.

Over several evenings he went to her front door,
waited in the hope that somebody would leave or enter

the house. When he had waited long enough or shouted until his voice was hoarse, he went to Gillett Square and either drank a lager at the bar below the Vortex or a small coffee at the Ethiopian coffee kiosk. Seated in the open air, the square as animated as ever, he scrutinised every passing female in the hope that one would be her, the woman who had just wanted to be held by a stranger one night.

Around mid-August, the weather changed and it rained for three consecutive days then stopped, but the sky remained overcast and grey. One afternoon Ralph picked up a note in the hallway of the house. It informed him that the teenage boy next door was planning to hold another party over the coming weekend. Ralph squashed up the note and binned it as soon as he got into his flat. At least the boy had chosen a weekend for his rave.

Ralph watched the boy erect the canvas tent in the back garden. The weekend arrived and with it intermittent showers. That Saturday, Ralph saw the boy pacing the garden as cumulus clouds swirled above, descending ever lower. He doubted that the party would happen and if it did, it wouldn't be as successful as the July effort. But Ralph did not intend to hang around to find out. As soon as the music started in the empty tent, he left the house and, through a light drizzle, headed towards Gillett Square.

He went to the house beside the railway line and shouted into the letterbox, but as on previous occasions there was no reply. He now noticed letters and junk mail strewn in the hallway. He walked back to Gillett Square and ordered a small coffee from the Ethiopian coffee place then sat on a damp chair at one of the tables and looked at the square. It was almost empty, and in the absence of people felt quite desolate. He could not finish his coffee.

He walked back home through a light rain that created a misty effect on the street and over the houses. The party next door was a non-event, though the boy insisted on playing music to himself while the rain fell.

Emotionally exhausted but high on coffee, Ralph slept fitfully and woke up at 12.50 a.m. He washed his face and left the house in search of COAC. He found the blue door in a mews behind the high street and wondered why she had taken such a circuitous route on the night they went there. He rang the bell and was admitted into the atrium where, as on his previous visit, all the tables were taken. He ordered a honey and ginger tea and walked to the rear room where they had sat listening to the calming and soporific music of the guitar player, scrutinising all the female faces as he passed. The table where they had sat was empty and he went there. Again he noticed the man in the fedora hat.

The entrance of any female made his heart beat faster but it was never her, Maria. He had been sitting there for fifteen minutes when a man – small and dark, with long brown incisors and a wisp of beard – approached him and said: 'I don't understand English society.' Ralph looked at him blankly as if to suggest that he was the last person on Earth from whom to seek enlightenment on a subject that was so clearly tormenting the questioner.

The man in the fedora hat came up behind the man and said something in a language unfamiliar to Ralph.

The man's face transmogrified into a mask of fear and he rushed away.

'Goodness, what did you tell him?' Ralph asked, standing up.

'I told him that he was a character who belonged in another story.'

Puzzled, Ralph said, 'Why should that make him so scared?'

'It's a polite way of saying "Go away, or I'll rub you out. Delete."'

'That's extreme.'

'I know, I know. My preference is to abandon my characters, not to delete them.'

Ralph looked at him blankly.

'You see, he's in the habit of asking all my customers the same question, then he gets aggressive.'

'So it's your business?'

'Sit down, Ralph,' the man said.

Startled, Ralph said, 'How do you know my name?'

'Oh, I saw you here with a friend of mine not long ago.'

'Maria? She's your friend? Where is she?'

'Don't worry, she'll be here soon.'

'How do you know that?'

The man thought for a moment then said, 'You could say I brought the two of you together.'

Ralph sat down and felt somewhat calmer, as if the man's reassurance that he would see Maria again was what he had been needing to hear. Questions buzzed in his mind.

'You know my name but I don't know yours,' he said.

'Pardon my manners.' The man reached into the pocket of his red brocaded waistcoat, pulled out a small silver case, flipped it open and took out a card which he handed to Ralph.

It read 'Idren Nninedfas'. He spelled out the unusual name, and added, 'Founder and Proprietor of COAC.'

He extended his right hand and Ralph shook it, and it felt firm and soft and warm.

'And what does COAC mean?'

The man smiled and said, 'She didn't tell you?'

'No.'

'I see. Maybe she doesn't know, either. COAC is an acronym. It means the Café of Abandoned Characters.'

'I see,' said Ralph.

'I am pleased that you're seeing with my eyes,' the man said, rising from his seat. 'Now I must abandon you to your fate. Enjoy the night.'

Ralph watched him walk away, bowing to people at the tables he passed, and as soon as he disappeared from view the small stage lit up, and the guitar player emerged and sat on a low stool. He tuned his guitar then started playing what sounded like 'Recuerdos de la Alhambra', though Ralph couldn't be sure because the music was so faint. The playing ended, nobody clapped.

Then the guitar player started again, and as the light grew dimmer, a woman – the spotlight trained on her feet, slowly danced into view on the stage. She proceeded to dance flamenco style, stomping her feet and swirling the hem of her dress, which was made of iridescent red feathers. The music reached a crescendo and she stomped her feet at a furious pace, providing an accompanying percussive sound. As the music subsided, the stage lights brightened, illuminating the flamenco dancer's face. It was a face that Ralph instantly recognised. He glanced down at the name card again, and understanding came to him in a brilliant flash. And he knew then with absolute and disturbing certainty where the evening and the rest of his life was going – because he now understood that this, all this craving and longing and searching, was his story.

Wet Sunday Morning Blues

Three days before I was due to attend Lucy Colhern's annual autumn party, I received a letter from the owner of the flat I was living in, informing me that he would be back in a month's time. He was in India, had gone there in search of inner peace, and his letter was mostly a panegyric on the soul-enriching experience of living on ten pence a day, saving its most devastating news for the last line. I'd been living in his Ladbroke Grove flat for over a year, and the prospect of uprooting myself yet again for my sixth move in three years plunged me into depression. Nonetheless, when Saturday night came, I found the energy to attend Lucy Colhern's party.

She lived nearby in an Italianate villa with a floating population of friends. A sybaritic heiress, androgynous in appearance, she was famous for holding parties that went on for days at a time. Her guests that night came from the four corners of the Earth, with a liberal sprinkling of Africans. The rich blend of esoteric world music reflected the cosmopolitan nature of the gathering, and the pièce de resistance consisted of the only known recording of the musical genius of an obscure people located on a tiny, remote island in Oceania. Called 'Symphony of the Dead

Souls', it was played on an instrument made from the 300-plus bones in the human body.

The following afternoon, still recovering from my drink and drug excesses in Lucy's house, I received a telephone call. I didn't recognise the voice on the other end of the line straight away, but once I heard the name, Kawan, I remembered the handsome bearded African with the barrel chest and bass-filled laughter I had met at Lucy's party. I remembered, too, that we had talked at length about African politics, and parted after swapping telephone numbers. I'd said that I didn't know how long I would be on my number because I was looking for somewhere to live. He was calling to tell me that he had a room to rent in his house.

Following his instructions, I made my way from Ladbroke Grove over to Hackney, to a London that was as strange to me as another city: narrow streets, countless council housing estates – even the sky seemed somehow lower, as if a permanent depression hung over this part of London. But my journey ended on a quiet, pleasant-looking street of Victorian artisans' cottages, which had obviously been colonised by the lower middle classes. The woman who answered the door of the house I called at was so beautiful that I stumbled to find my opening words.

She introduced herself as Olivia, invited me in, and in the kitchen explained that Kawan had been called away on urgent business. (I would soon discover the reason for his frequent absences from the house.) Her accent evoked images of tea on an English village green, encircled by oaks and elms, on a summer Sunday afternoon; of men dressed in white linen suits and women in pale floral-patterned dresses, all watching a cricket match in progress.

She showed me the room, which was on the first floor. It was perfectly adequate for my needs. A transit point. And the house had a good feel.

She offered me tea after my brief inspection of the room. And as we chatted at the kitchen table, she mentioned that she had seen me at Lucy Colhern's party. I was surprised because I had absolutely no memory of her, yet I was certain that, once seen, Olivia was not easily forgotten. Her luxuriant brown hair, her pale blue eyes, her graceful poise – and that incredible accent and fluent speech – those were the memories I took away. Enchanted by Olivia, I even forgot to ask about the rent. Was she a neighbour? Kawan's girlfriend?

I was out of Ladbroke Grove and in Hackney within a week. The rent was not unreasonably high or charitably low, and had been settled in a discussion in which Kawan participated as if money was a distasteful subject, included in our arrangement only because necessity demanded it.

My curiosity about Olivia was quickly satisfied. She was, to my disappointment but greater relief, Kawan's girlfriend, and she lived in the house. In Kawan's company, Olivia's beauty appeared somehow diminished, less radiant, commonplace even. Before Kawan's next lengthy absence, the three of us often went out together, to parties, restaurants – and it never failed to intrigue me how bland, characterless and almost invisible Olivia seemed beside Kawan.

Years later, I now recognise Olivia as the sort of woman who, skilled in the art of self-effacement, elects to project and conceal her beauty at will. If she seemed like a pale carnation in Kawan's lapel, a tasteful tie, an adornment that enhanced his natural regality, that was the role she chose for herself. And that was her power.

At the outset, it was Kawan who commanded my attention, loyalty and affection. We often sat up late into the night, discussing politics and women and love. We disagreed with sufficient frequency to sustain many late nights, oiling our conversation with beer, wine and scotch. It was on one such night that I discovered that his princely bearing was not an affectation; he wasn't just another African in London posing as a prince. He had lived as a prince until his early teens, when a military coup ushered in leaders uncompromisingly committed to republican rule. The soldiers had sent his entire family into exile, and his father had died in an Earl's Court flat after falling out with Kawan's mother. Kawan was attending an English public school at the time. He had not been home to Kanji in twenty years.

Kawan did not seem to feel bitter towards the soldiers, who were themselves ousted a year later in a violent coup. Nor was he without hope of one day returning to the land of his birth, to the land surrounded by seven lakes where flame-red flamingoes fed, and tilapia fish grew in magnificent abundance. But there were days when his hope was wrapped in a cocoon of melancholia and the royal future seemed self-delusional. On such occasions we would talk about our disgust with life, the senselessness of suicide; or maybe we would talk about the sweet and wounding loves we had known and lost. The next day, the prince would re-emerge, his belief that he would one day take his rightful place on the throne in the country surrounded by seven lakes restored and implacable.

Olivia sometimes stayed up to play Scrabble with us, but always retired by eleven. I'd begun to notice a subtle unease between her and Kawan, but did not attach much importance to it until early one evening, reading in my room, I heard Olivia scream, followed by steps rushing up the stairs, then Kawan shouting angrily, 'Come back here!' I heard her fall, then I heard her scream for Kawan to stop. At this point I opened my room door and saw Olivia on the floor, pressed against the wall, her skirt riding up on her thighs, her navy-blue tights torn around her knee, exposing skin several shades lighter than on her face, her hands raised against Kawan's raised fist.

'Kawan, don't!' I shouted.

My voice must have broken some spell, driven his fury away. Olivia scrambled up, sobbing, and ran to her room and locked the door. Kawan did not look at me; he hung his head and walked slowly back downstairs.

Later that evening, I took a break from a collection of Somerset Maugham short stories I'd been reading, left my room and went down the silent stairs to the kitchen. I found Kawan sitting at the table, a half-empty bottle of whisky in front of him, a tall glass in his hand. Remorse and frustrated anger were as palpable as the scent of the whisky.

Kawan invited me into his study, a ground-floor room lined with books, periodicals, folders and music albums. It also contained a mini-stereo, a small television, an armchair convertible into a single bed and a leather-bound swivel chair at a desk strewn with papers. Engaged in a rambling conversation, I knew I would not get back to my room until dawn.

We did not talk about the altercation or Olivia.

Somewhere in that night, speaking in a tone of apology, Kawan told me this puzzling creation story.

'In the beginning, God made holes in the earth, and from one came man, from another woman. God gave them land to cultivate, a pick, an axe, a pot, plates and millet. He told them to cultivate the land, to sow it with millet, to build a dwelling and to cook their food in it. Instead of carrying out God's instructions, they ate the millet raw, broke the plates, put dirt in their pot and then went and hid in the forest. Seeing that he had been disobeyed, God called upon a he-monkey and a she-monkey and gave them the same tools and instructions. They worked, cooked and ate the millet. And God was pleased. So He cut off the monkeys' tails and fastened them to the man and woman, saying to the monkeys, "Be men" and to the humans, "Be monkeys."'

The Hackney night faded, giving way to an overcast dawn visible through the east-facing window. I decided to go to bed. As I was leaving the room, Kawan stopped me by placing an arm on my shoulder. When I looked at him he said nothing, and for what seemed like a long time he looked into my eyes and I sensed his loneliness and his fear, felt those emotions as sharply as if they were my own. I sensed that there was much that he wanted to say, from a heart that had known the remotest corners of pain, sensed that he was inviting me to travel to those territories with him.

We parted awkwardly on that grey dawn.

Soon afterwards, Kawan began to spend days away from the house. Olivia, who I had seen only once since the fight, became equally scarce. When Kawan was absent, she left for work early in the morning and seldom got back before late evening, by which time I was usually ensconced in my room reading. It was as though our little community had been irreparably shattered. Nonetheless I was aware that Kawan and Olivia were again on good terms. He would return home late at night, and I often heard his gentle knock on Olivia's door. From my window I saw him leave the house a few times, long after Olivia had gone to work, and noticed how he seemed to steal away, as if departing the home of a mistress.

One Friday evening, Kawan invited me out for a drink. I set off expecting to chase the night – a vice we shared – but found myself in a vast apartment in St John's Wood watching dignified elderly men prostrate themselves before Kawan, who accepted these acts of obeisance with calm. On the way there he had explained that a delegation from the royal court had been negotiating with his country's ruling military junta to restore the monarchy. There had been a major breakthrough, and Kawan would soon be travelling home on an exploratory trip. It was strange to see these old men venerate my friend and landlord in that opulent apartment with its pink-upholstered Victorian wing chairs; stranger still to see the transformation their veneration wrought on him: the almost imperceptible change from being princely to being a prince.

From the moment Kawan took his seat in the giant leather club chair, people began appearing; they had been waiting for his arrival. As they rose from the floor after greeting him, they would intone words in his language (later he would explain that they were praising the royal house) and he would hold a brief conversation with the supplicant. Some of the old men went to stand behind Kawan, their grey heads bowed. They were then followed by a younger group. Among them were beautiful women, whose skins were as smooth and dark as polished black coral.

We remained in that apartment without sleep until the middle of the next morning. Despite having spent over twelve hours greeting people and discussing the state of politics with elderly men, who I discovered were his advisers and, at times, I sensed, his prison wardens, Kawan did not seem tired. Indeed, he glowed with an aura of contentment that was partially obscured by the occasional signs of boredom he let slip.

There was much that I wanted to ask him in the taxi as we were driven back to Hackney from the salubrious surroundings of St John's Wood. But, unable to decide where to start, I held my tongue and wondered instead whether Kawan had always led this double life between tradition and the present, between the sacred and the profane, between the African he was born and the sort of Englishman he had become.

Two weeks later, Kawan left the country. He said he would be away for four months.

Olivia and I did not immediately become friends. For some weeks we met each other briefly in the kitchen, exchanged greetings and terse observations about the weather. Then one wet Sunday afternoon, when we were both in the house, we spent many hours at the kitchen table talking about books, movies and the countries we had visited. Soon we started meeting for breakfast, and again in the evening, and slowly the gloom that had settled over the house since Kawan's departure began to lift. No matter how late we stayed up, we went to our separate rooms, though I often felt it was an unusual conclusion to the evening. And the more those evenings took place, the deeper I fell in love with Olivia.

So, when she invited me out for a drink with two of her female friends – Sue and Helen, both white and English – I accepted without hesitation. I had by then made a few friends in Hackney and, not wishing to be alone in the company of Olivia's friends, invited a friend called Jack Baines along. We met in the White Horse pub on a Friday night.

As closing time approached, a squat muscular man, his head covered in a woollen hat, came to our table and greeted Olivia. She gave him a broad easy smile and introduced him as Sylvester, then went off to the bar with him. Jealousy and curiosity swirled inside me. When she came back, Olivia revealed that Sylvester had invited us all to a blues dance. By now we had been drinking for hours and had reached that state of intoxication that made any suggestion of extending our drinking irresistibly attractive. The five of us followed Sylvester to a basement several blocks from the pub.

I remember little about the sequence of events in that low-ceilinged basement, only that it filled up swiftly after we arrived. I saw Olivia dancing a blues dance with Sylvester, which showed that she was no stranger to this subterranean world. I saw her elegantly clothed body pressed against Sylvester's weightlifter's mass and watched her twist and writhe in sensual movements. I did not see Olivia leave, and when I noticed that she was nowhere to be seen, I felt agitated. Her friends were less concerned than me; we all left the blues dance around 3 a.m. and went our separate ways.

When I got back, I saw a light under Olivia's door. She was home. I knocked and asked if she was all right, hoping that she would open the door but fearful of what would happen if she did. She simply shouted back that she was fine, and I went to bed.

The following day, as we stood in the kitchen, Olivia asked me to promise not to mention anything about the evening to Kawan. I said I wouldn't and, besides, I hadn't seen anything improper, unless she considered her blues dancing skills an impropriety, which I certainly didn't. So the night at the blues dance became our secret, and this secret our bond.

Over the next few weeks my desire for Olivia grew stronger, became a restless beast and threatened to break free from the platonic screen I had erected between us out of loyalty to Kawan. My nights were a tormented struggle between my conscience and my heart. On two consecutive nights, unable to sleep, I left my room and stealthily approached Olivia's door, intending to knock, to ask her to admit me into her bed. But always, at the last moment, I shrank back at the possibility of rejection, the possibility of betrayal, the possibility of success. When we met in the kitchen or on the stairs, I averted my eyes and feigned busyness.

Finally, I decided that I could not remain in the house with her any longer, and with frenzied resolution set about finding somewhere else to live. Three months after Kawan's departure I moved out, to a squalid room in Finsbury Park. Here I attempted to and eventually succeeded in regaining my equanimity.

I telephoned Kawan's house about a month after his expected return. He answered the phone in a slow, lazy voice. I arranged to visit him, hoping to see Olivia again. The Kawan I met was plumper and more majestic in appearance, but he was in the grip of a deep gloom. Olivia had moved out; he had returned to an empty house.

I was shocked. Olivia had given me no indication that she was planning on leaving. In fact, when I had told her I was moving out, she said she would be lonely until Kawan got back. But in my conversation with Kawan that night I discovered that he and Olivia had been involved in a long and painful relationship from which each had been trying to escape. Kawan told me about Sylvester, the dreadlocked weightlifter: two years previously, Olivia had had an affair with him, and she and Kawan had almost parted as a result of that transgression. When Kawan mentioned Sylvester he did so with utter scorn in his voice, which gave me the impression that he objected less to Olivia having had an affair and more to the social status of her chosen lover. She had wounded him by choosing a man who was obviously below his stature. And that had made her action infra dig.

He explained that on the night of their fight – not their first – he had been trying once again to explain to her why her action was wrong; trying to describe the peculiar and specific way in which she had wounded him. But she had not understood, or had feigned incomprehension. He said that he was the first African Olivia had known, and that it was he who had introduced her to the world of the blues dance, which, for a brief moment in his life, had helped to soothe the pain of his long, long exile. Olivia, he said, made no distinction between the West Indian 'roughnecks' in the neighbourhood and somebody like him. A prince.

Yet when I asked him if he had intended to marry Olivia and take her home as his queen, Kawan looked at me aghast. Marrying Olivia had never been an option. His wife would be chosen for him by the royal elders – the old men I had seen prostrating themselves at his feet. His would be a bride from a select family. Not because – he stressed with painful sincerity – because that was the way he wanted it, but because that was how the king of his people married. Olivia had always known that one day, his destiny would be fulfilled; he did not own his life.

We talked until after midnight, and I decided to sleep in Kawan's house rather than make my way back to

Finsbury Park. Later that night, I was awoken by Kawan shouting 'Olivia, Olivia, Olivia!' as he wandered from one end of the ground floor to another. I went downstairs and met him in the hallway. His face looked pained, his eyes watery. 'She's gone, she's gone,' he said.

'But you always knew it would end like this,' I said.

'No,' he said. 'No. She promised to stay here in this house, to be available for me whenever I came back to London. I believed her.'

A violent spasm shook him and the tears he had been holding back flooded out. Involuntarily, I held him, and he rested his head on my shoulder. We stayed that way for a minute or so then parted. He went into his study and I returned to bed. By the following morning he had regained his regal composure. The incident in the night seemed like a dream.

A month later, Kawan travelled to Kanji. I read in the newspapers of the restoration of the monarchy in his country. A year passed, during which I had moved to yet another part of London, and I read of the coronation of Kawan as the King of Kanji.

It is many years since those events took place, and over the years I have heard from mutual friends that Olivia married a stockbroker and moved to Surrey. I last saw Kawan when he came to London for a medical check-up, something to do with his heart. Some days, especially on rainy Sunday mornings, I think of them, Olivia and Kawan, of their doomed love, of my own tortured feelings for Olivia, and I know then that there are people sadder than a wet Sunday morning.

The Unfinished Tapestry

That February night, at an hour when an icy mist smothered the marshes and surrounding streets of terraced houses and housing estates, Estelle Hardwood was as wide awake as the cats that prowled the frozen back gardens. She was sitting up in bed, her lower half beneath the pink candlewick bedspread, working with a sense of quiet urgency on a tapestry of flowers and trees she had started to make years ago. She had often put aside this piece of work to stitch or knit smaller and less elaborate gifts for the steady stream of grandchildren and great-grandchildren who flowed from her own prodigious motherhood. But in five months' time she was due to fly back to Jamaica, to a retirement house there; and she was determined to finish this tapestry before leaving England. A framed photograph of the house awaiting her presence stood under the bedside lamp, and when her concentration lapsed she gazed at it for inspiration to continue her weaving until a few hours before dawn.

Suddenly, the silence was shattered. The doorbell rang and an urgent voice called out: 'Mum, Mum, it's me.' She would recognise that voice even from her grave as belonging to her youngest child and son, Roy.

She put aside the tapestry, slipped on her dressing gown and went to open the door. The parked cars were covered in a luminous patina of frost and she glimpsed the white tower blocks across the road, mist swirling around their illuminated peaks like sea mist around a lighthouse. She heard an owl hoot as it flew towards the marshes that lay behind the towers, and the paludal chill caused her to shiver.

Roy, leaning heavily on his walking stick, hobbled past her into the house. She closed the door. Silently, she took the leather beret from him and helped him remove his grey greatcoat. When he had finished, still leaning on his walking stick, he hugged Estelle in a powerful and tremulous embrace, enveloped her slim straight figure in his solid bulky mass like a mighty fist clasping a pen. Glued to him for an instant, feeling the violent throbbing of his heart, she remembered the day when she first held him in her arms.

She pulled away from Roy and probed his face. His sweaty, lined forehead told her he had struggled through the cold damp night to visit her. She looked deeply into his cloudy eyes and saw that he was in pain, and she felt afraid because for many years she had secretly feared that she would live to bury him.

He was the youngest of her eleven children, the boy who had burst from her womb, demanding life, when she was forty years old and less than a year in England, as if crossing the Atlantic Ocean had restored her fertility, as if the Almighty had sent her a gift of consolation for the trauma of travelling, the uncertainty of arrival, the difficulties of starting a new life in a strange land.

The gas fire hissed as Estelle solemnly settled her visitor into the chair opposite the glass cabinet of sporting trophies, which stood against a wall covered in framed black and white photographs of her wedding, and colour photographs of her children's weddings. On another wall, among photographs of grand- and great-grandchildren, hung one of her earliest efforts at stitching a tapestry. She brought him tea, and he laced it with whisky from a silver flask he kept in the breast pocket of his jacket.

'How is your leg?' she asked.

'February. Cruel month. Take more painkillers in February than any other time of year.' He was leaning forward on the chair, clasping the top of the stick. 'See you still got my medals and cups and trophies,' he said, a wry smile on his face.

Estelle looked at the silver cups, shields, medals and wooden plaques. Roy had won them all in boxing and football competitions before he turned twenty-one. They were crammed on three shelves and spilled out onto the top of the cabinet. She used to polish them once a year, but it had been several months since she had noticed them, and now that Roy's presence forced her to scrutinise them, their dullness disconcerted her. They were long overdue for a good polish.

'Manda came to see me the middle of last month,' Roy said.

Estelle knew instantly why Roy, stricken with thrombosis and other afflictions with names that defied her memory – afflictions that required him to take a daily cocktail of prescribed drugs – had hauled himself through the cold streets at this ungodly hour to see her. Manda, her eldest and most faithful daughter, was handling the travel arrangements, which would include a farewell party for all the family. She, Estelle, was seventy-five years old and believed she had ten to fifteen years of life left. Her own mother and grandmother had lived to be centenarians, but she did not expect to live that long. Settling in England had been an ordeal, an ordeal that had robbed her of her husband, killed in a car accident five years after they arrived. But she was not bitter; she had done her best in life and her eleven children were proof of that achievement. Now she just wanted the peace and tranquility of the little house in Portland. Manda had already posted off her application for a Jamaican passport, and next month the 'For Sale' sign would be erected on the front garden wall. In June one of her daughters in Canada would visit the island to ensure that all was ready for her arrival in July.

'Manda told me you're going home and it got me thinking about my trophies,' Roy said.

Estelle said, 'Manda offered to look after them, and I am wondering whether it makes sense carrying them all that way.'

He looked to the floor and indirectly at her, and she saw she had hurt his feelings, saw that beneath his bulky manhood, his hardened face, his card player's unsmiling smile, he was still a fragile little boy.

He said, 'Don't leave them behind, Mum. Take them with you. I won them for you.'

'I know you did, Roy, I know,' she said. She wondered whether there would be enough space in the container for all her belongings, the sofa and the armchairs, the bed and the wardrobe, the fridge and the cooker and now Roy's trophies.

Roy rose with a great effort, as if he had been seated for days and his joints had rusted or seized up. He went to the cabinet and ran his eyes over the cups and shields. Then he picked up the largest cup, which was too large to fit into the cabinet and so sat on top of it.

'Never forget this fight,' he said, staring at the dullish silver. 'Against a southpaw, Sonny Speedy Shanks. He was good. Fast. He had me against the ropes in the sixth round. I was struggling to stay on my feet. Just couldn't stop those combination punches and I couldn't land one. Was going to go down until I thought of you, how I really wanted to win that fight for you. And for a second or two, I imagined that you were in the ring with me, and it was you who guided my fist to slip that upper cut through his defences, and when it struck, it struck good and true, and I knew I'd hurt him, hurt him good, hurt him proper. He backed off quickly. I didn't have the energy to follow it up but I got him again in the next round, couple of jabs, and in the one after that I got him good, bam in the middle of his chin. A sweet win. Sweet.'

Roy stood tall and proud on his three legs and seemed to examine his clenched fist.

Estelle listened in silence as Roy picked up another, lesser trophy and started reminiscing about the fight for which he had won that one. Behind Estelle's silence lay self-reproach and remorse. None of her four boys had amounted to much in England, in this sprawling, never-ending city called London, in this forever damp neighbourhood on the edge of Hackney Marshes. None had had Roy's courage, but they still had their health, and unlike Roy, they lived normal, happy family lives. She regarded him as her biggest failure. Why? She often felt she had loved him too much because he had entered her life at a trying moment when she needed somebody to love, and when her other children had outgrown the quality of loving that her heart was bursting to give. And in loving him too much she had made him feel invincible, beyond defeat.

Roy had ignored medical warnings and continued boxing long after developing the blood clot in his leg that would eventually hospitalise him. When the boxing authorities seized his licence, he resorted to bare-knuckle midnight boxing matches on the marshes, or in back-street warehouses. Released from hospital, he had drifted into a bad crowd, taken to gambling and running an illegal nightclub, a shebeen or blues dance or whatever you call it, a place of such ill-repute, such infamy, that some Sundays she was ashamed to show her face in church. Everybody knew about Roy.

Now Roy hobbled back to his chair and lowered himself into it. The excitement of remembering and his brief exertion had tired him. He smiled and said with playful petulance: 'Don't know why you want to go back to that little island. What're you going to do there?'

'Keep a little garden, go to church, and we still have plenty relatives there.'

'What about all your grandchildren and great-grandchildren? How many are there now?'

'Lost count. Used to keep a little notebook of birthdays. Can't keep up any more. Twenty-four between here and New York and Toronto. Fifteen great-grandchildren, another one soon come, too.'

'I'm the only one who hasn't given you any,' Roy said flatly, his eyes fixed on the cabinet of trophies.

'There's still time,' Estelle said. 'You're not even forty yet. You're still a young man. You just need to go to church and find yourself a nice young lady ...'

Estelle suddenly became aware that Roy seemed blurred, as if she were seeing him through sleepy eyes or through frosted glass. From her chair she could hardly make out his face; only his voice told her she was speaking to her youngest child.

'I used to think I had plenty of time but I don't think so any more,' Roy said. He sounded faint and distant.

While Estelle was wondering how to reply, Roy stood up, his indistinct mass rocking unsteadily like a tree whose roots have not properly penetrated the soil and so it is easily bent by a strong wind.

'Got to go now,' he said. 'I know it won't be easy to take the cups but I didn't win them easily. For my sake, don't leave them behind.'

'Don't worry, Roy, they won't leave me.'

'Thank you, Mum, thank you.'

His voice was so weak she was not certain she was talking to a living person. Alarmed, she rose and went to him and she was relieved to be able to touch his face, to feel its dry texture, its contours; but she almost recoiled at its cold stiffness. She helped him on with his greatcoat and beret.

Before going through the door, back into the cold foggy night, he hugged her again and said in what sounded like a whisper, 'Goodbye, Mum. I love you.'

She watched him go through the gate. Then he was gone, as if swallowed by the fog, and long after his departure Estelle continued to hear an eerie, disturbing echo of finality, like the silence after a hurricane has spent its fury.

On the evening of the following day, Maurice, the third-born of Estelle's four sons, brought news of Roy's death from cardiac arrest. Estelle received this tragic news with an outward calm. But over the following days, as more details emerged, when she heard the estimated time of Roy's death – she initially thought he had over-exerted himself visiting her late at night – then she became convinced she had spoken to Roy's ghost and took to her bed. From there she telephoned Manda, for only Manda would believe and could comfort her.

The cremation took place some weeks later, on a Friday night, followed by a noisy reception in the community hall on the Nightingale Estate. For the first time in many years all the Hardwoods living in England were gathered under one roof, and Vinette, one of Estelle's daughters who lived in New York, came over. To their numbers were added Roy's many friends and their families, black and white, who all had the pasty or light-shy appearance of people who seldom ventured outside in the daylight hours; many had gold-capped teeth and wore chunky gold chains round their necks, and on their fingers were matching rings that looked more like weapons than jewellery. They delivered lengthy speeches that praised Roy's courage and generosity, and repeatedly referred to him as 'a warrior', which made his mother wonder what war he had been fighting.

Estelle occupied the central position on the main table. Her daughters tended to her every need, and in between receiving condolences from strangers, she comforted and hugged and kissed a tribe of grandchildren and great-grandchildren, who were oblivious to the solemnity of the occasion. Far from being a mournful day, there was much laughter and gaiety, like the Christmas gatherings of the past when all the family came together.

When Estelle was at last alone in her bedroom, she reflected on Roy's funeral. She had spoken to more people in one day than she had done in two years, yet she did not feel tired. Roy's brothers Dexter and Laurence, and their wives and children, so many grown children now, had all seemed well, though it concerned her that Laurence was out of work and separated from his wife. Her daughters Rose and Pansy and Manda and their husbands and children seemed happier than her sons' families. But Rose's youngest daughter, her namesake, Estelle, seemed so miserable; she would have to invite her round one Sunday afternoon, bake a sweet-potato pudding for the occasion. And one of her great-granddaughters, Debbie, had just given birth to a boy whom she had named Roy – Estelle's very first great-great-grandchild. Something wrong there, a mere child the mother. But she, Estelle, wouldn't ask too many questions; just knit a shawl for baby Roy. Which reminded her that she needed a tin of silver polish for Roy's trophies.

With these thoughts playing in her mind, she gazed at the colour photograph of the retirement house in Jamaica, looked long and hard at it. Before Roy's death, that picture of a house she had never actually seen would make her imagine that she could smell the fragrance of ripe mangoes, feel the warm breeze blowing off the sea, hear the cicadas in the night, see the green hills behind the house. No amount of concentration could produce those effects now. Instead, she continued to hear the laughter and cries of the children, to smell the raw overpowering earth like the scent of the newly born great-great-grandchild whom she had cradled in her arms and rocked to sleep.

She reached over and turned the photograph face down. Then she picked up the unfinished tapestry and held it under the bedside lamp, where the light revealed several flaws she had not noticed before. She decided it would be beautiful when finished, but she would have to correct those bad stitches. Yes, much work remained to be undone and redone.

She picked up her needle.

The Zaria Walkman

Zaria, Kaduna State, Northern Nigeria
'In my view,' said Professor Gbenga, 'the chap is probably a primeval reaction against the ubiquitous trends of modernity and development. He's a stoical opponent of that which we, this whole community, represent: progress.' The prof leaned back into his chair as his left hand swept expansively across the Zaria night sky. He inhaled on his curving brown pipe, and a discernible smugness settled on his rotund face.

They sat in the Senior Staff Club: behind them, the swimming pool made gentle lapping sounds. Kufena rock was barely visible through the dense darkness, and on the table stood numerous empty bottles of beer – monuments to a night of drinking and talking.

'That's nonsense,' said Haruna with an alcohol-induced arrogance that bordered on insolence. 'There's a clear and simple description of the man's behaviour: insanity, dementia, call it what you wish. As part of the progress you champion, this place needs an asylum for his kind ...'

'Prof's got an interesting point,' Saidu interjected. 'In fact, I should invite the guy to give a couple of special lectures on my course: "Social change in Nigeria, a view from the streets". How about that as a title?'

The group laughed at Saidu's humour. Several rounds of beer and endless dishes of suya in the cool night air had clearly fostered a sense of mirth amongst them. Only Sule remained quiet. His bloodshot eyes betrayed the sleepy effects of the beer, but he listened with concealed interest.

The topic of discussion was a local character who daily perambulated between Zaria and the university campus – a distance of some twenty kilometres. He was of medium height, dark with the shade of the Birom people from Plateau State, and walked with the proud, erect carriage of a soldier. From his face and body, his age could have been around thirty or slightly younger. He was distinguished from other pedestrians by his unabashed nudity, although he sometimes hung a coarse, military-type blanket around his shoulders. Under the heat of the savannah sun he would march from one point to another in what seemed like senseless journeys.

Smiling like a youthful disputant about to deliver the final blow to a tiresome opponent, Professor Gbenga replied, 'Your reaction is quite typical, Haruna. It differs little from that of the fellow's contemporaries, and it's entirely consistent with your approach to knowledge. You leave no room for speculation. You want to pigeon-hole the man's behaviour in one of two boxes, normal or abnormal. I, at least, elevate him above those sterile categories. That pedantic dichotomy. My theory bestows dignity on him and the unknown cause for which he fights. Who knows? Perhaps the site of the campus was once of some cultural significance that has disappeared with progress. If so, his trips could be seen as a noble, if futile, attempt to reunite past and present.'

'Hah,' Haruna scoffed, took a swig from the bottle and went on, 'and *that* reaction is so typical of you bourgeois academics. Reality stares you straight in the face, but you choose to explain it away with metaphysical speculations. The man is mad. He's mad because the progress that you represent – not me, for I sometimes think I am a victim, too – has driven him mad.

'It's the car,' he carried on. 'It's that expensive stretch of tarmac built for only a few. It's this university, the purpose of which remains alien to the people around us; they can't penetrate it. The man's unique only for the form by which his madness finds expression – pointless journeys between A and B. There are many others like him, but they are not as conspicuous. Nonetheless, they're victims of your neo-colonial bourgeois progress, your mad rush to catch up with the ex-colonial master.'

Hearing this, the prof released a deep sonorous laughter, as though Haruna had tickled his chest. Even Sule had woken up on hearing the passion in Haruna's voice. The professor was an old hat at debating. He could make even the most serious remarks of his opponents seem like jokes. He excelled at the art of ridiculing others, especially those younger than himself. Yet it was all done with such good humour that he pulled it off each time.

Exchanges of this kind were common in the Senior Staff Club and regular Saturday-night parties. Haruna was a new breed of young academic. Although comfortable in the university environs, he spoke up for the downtrodden and oppressed. Saidu, when serious, also claimed to be a radical, but most often he blew the wind of mischief couched in the language of the academic community. The professor, American-educated, was of a different age. His interest in the world beyond the campus wall was purely abstract. His mind seemed to be forever floating in a cloud of ideas, of possible connections between observed events.

'Prof,' Saidu said, 'there's a widespread rumour that your noble savage was once a student of yours. Apparently, so the rumour goes, he repeated your African Philosophy course for three years, and the continuous failure proved too much for his fragile brain.'

'Saidu,' the prof said heartily, 'why don't you go and get us some more beer? That way you won't be here to make your asinine remarks.'

By the time Saidu returned to the table, the conversation had changed to the recent government measures to curb corruption. Another heated exchange ensued between Haruna and Professor Gbenga. Sule, enlivened by a fresh bottle of beer, threw in the opinions of an American-trained economist.

As always they parted amicably. The professor went home to his English wife, Saidu to his mistress – a beautiful Caribbean lecturer – Sule to his nearby flat, where he lived alone, and Haruna, because he wanted to live among 'the common people – the talakawas' – had a long lonely journey to Sabon Gari.

Haruna was drunk, a state in which he had often driven home on the mostly straight road, and he knew all its bends, even on a moonless night. He laughed as he recalled the professor's views on the Zaria walkman. A noble savage indeed. The prof, he thought, needed to taste life beyond the campus walls; life with its insecurities, uncertainties and brutalities, its sheer wretchedness. All combined to drive people into the depths of insanity. We academics, thought Haruna, we cry when there are power cuts, or when water doesn't come. But this is nothing compared to what most people go through. Someone should deprive the professor of all his luxuries. Yes, let him taste life beyond the campus walls.

Suddenly Haruna's foot crashed on the brakes. Someone was in the middle of the road. He slowed the car to a crawling pace. It was a man. A stark naked man. His ebony skin glowed in the headlights, and he was dragging the carcass of a dead goat out of the road.

An uncontrollable wave of disgust swept over Haruna. He had been brought up as a Muslim, and although he now considered himself an atheist, he retained an aversion to unclean meat.

The naked man heaved the carcass to the roadside, stared at it for a moment, then in one swift move slung it over his shoulder and started towards Zaria. As he walked, his naked torso was bathed in the headlights, the goat's body bouncing up and down on his back, streams of blood flowing over his buttocks.

Suddenly galvanised into action, Haruna parked the car, leaving the lights on, and followed the Zaria walkman. A trailer flashed past. Haruna wondered what he would do on catching up with the man. He didn't know, but he continued his silent pursuit.

Finally the man turned into a clearing at the roadside. Fearing that he would lose him in the bush, Haruna started running. As he entered the bush, a heavy hand descended on his shoulder. It belonged to the Zaria walkman.

'Why are you following me?' asked the man in flawless English.

For an instant Haruna lost his voice, but regained his composure enough to stutter, 'What have you done with the dead animal? It's unclean, you know that?'

'What concern is it of yours?' the man said, releasing Haruna.

Haruna, dazed by the realisation that the Zaria walkman was no madman, and frightened by the man's calm and firm voice, wrestled with himself to understand the situation he had placed himself in. Why had he pursued the man? After all, it was no business of his what other people ate. The animal, although killed by a car, would probably make an excellent meal.

'None, none,' said Haruna, facing the man for the first time. 'But tell me,' he went on, his courage now fully retrieved from the midst of the disturbing encounter, 'why do you walk from Zaria to the campus day in, day out?'

The man's eyes seemed to glow. 'Why do you ask such a question?'

'Because,' said Haruna, 'I am, like most people in the university, curious.'

'You have answered your own questions,' the man retorted.

'I don't understand.'

'Neither do I, but I am also curious enough to want to understand.'

'What understanding can you gain from these pointless journeys of yours?'

'Is it not sufficient that I'm curious, that I want to understand?'

'To understand what?'

'To understand the question that needs to be asked.'

'You mean you're looking for a question?'

'Yes.'

'What does the question concern? Is it Zaria?'

'Had I a clue to the question, I could then start looking for the answer. But if the question has taken me this long to find – over five years and I have still not found it – then the answer will take the rest of my life.'

Perplexed by the man's logic, Haruna thought he should try a different line of questioning.

'When you're walking, what do you see?'

'I see you?'

'I don't mean now, other times.'

'I see you. I see questions, many, many questions, but not the right question – just as you ask the wrong questions.' So saying, he leapt into the bush and disappeared.

Haruna could only hear the sound of twigs breaking under the fleeing feet, and smell the odour of perspiration on the night air.

Haruna did not go home that night. Instead, he drove to an all-night bar in Sabon Gari. There he drank until solidly drunk. He crawled home after abandoning any efforts to start his car. For three nights and days he moped around his apartment, living on beer and local gin. He entertained no visitors. His friends' knocks on his door went unanswered.

When he finally reappeared, Haruna's friends and colleague saw a changed man. Even the usually apathetic students noticed the changes. His lectures were now always brief, invariably filled with cynical remarks about progress and history, and often concluded with the statement: 'One must find the right question.' Sometime he wandered along the faculty corridors muttering to himself, 'In pursuit of the right question'.

Then he started neglecting his appearance, became violently anti-social and finally disappeared from circulation.

There are now two Zaria walkmen: one walks on the left side from Zaria to the campus, the other on the right side. Sometimes they stand and stare at each other, as if they were deadly enemies. Only recently the police jailed both of them – in separate cells – for fighting over the carcass of a roadkill goat. Both were reported to be well educated, when they chose to talk.

Acknowledgements

The following stories, tweaked for this collection, first appeared elsewhere: 'The Zaria Walkman', *African Concord*, 1984; 'The Unfinished Tapestry', BBC Radio Four, *Morning Story*, 1994; 'The Black and White Museum', *Kunapipi*, 1998 and *Critical Quarterly*, 1999; 'Wet Sunday Morning Blues' (previously titled 'Rainy Sunday Morning Blues'), *IC3:Penguin Collection of Black British Writing, Eds., C. Newland & K. Sesay*, 2000.

Many thanks to my editor Pete Ayrton for his critical comments on some of the stories.